Smoky Mountain K-9

Foggy Mountain Intrigue

Book Five

Ashley A Quinn

TCA Publishing LLC

Smoky Mountain K-9

Copyright © 2023 by Ashley A Quinn

ISBN is 978-1-959943-02-0
Library of Congress Control Number: 2023900439

Printed in the United State of America

AUTHOR'S NOTE

Hello, all! Thank you for reading *Smoky Mountain K-9*. If you've read my work before, you know I strive to make my books as believable as possible. For this novel, I wanted to highlight the interaction between a K-9 handler and his dog, as well as how police dog training differs from traditional dog training. One of the ways I did that was to use the German commands a K-9 handler would use. I made sure to define each word the first time I used it, so it was clear what Carter was asking of Maverick, but subsequent uses may or may not be defined. To help with that, I've included a reference guide below. I hope you enjoy the book!

Happy reading!
    -Ashley

Attack: Fass (fahs)
Let Go: Aus (ow-ss)
Go: Lauf (low-f)
No: Nein (Nine)
Stay: Bleib (blibe)

Here/Come: Hier (hee-r)
Sit: Sitz (zitz)
Down: Platz (plah-tz)
Here/Come: Hier (hee-r)
Heel: Fuss (foos)
Track: Such (zook)
Guard: Pass Auf (pass-owf)
Quiet: Ruhig (Roo-ig)

ONE

The thump of the electronic dance beat coming from the speakers reverberated in Mara Roth's chest. She couldn't believe she let herself get talked into coming to this thing. It was one thing to agree to host the Valentine's bachelor auction at the equestrian center, but it was quite another to be part of the audience. She hadn't planned to come, but her friend, Brooke McGinty, showed up on her doorstep a half hour before the auction started and told her to change clothes, and she wasn't taking no for an answer. Mara tried to protest, anyway, but Brooke threatened to call their other friend, Gemma Davidson, who was co-conspirator for the auction benefitting the Foggy Mountain Women's Crisis Center.

At that point, Mara knew resistance was futile, so she changed into a black party dress and let Brooke usher her into the passenger seat of her car.

This was fun, though. She'd expected to feel out of place—she wasn't in the market for a man. But a lot of the women here had come in small groups, with only one of them bidding. Once Mara noticed that, she relaxed and started to enjoy herself. Some of these guys were total hams and worked the stage for all they were worth. It was great to see so much money raised for such a good cause.

"Okay, ladies. Next up we have Carter Townsend. He's Ferris County's K-9 deputy." The emcee's voice rose over the music. She held out an arm, gesturing to the man emerging from behind the curtain.

Mara's eyes rounded, and a tingle went through her lady parts. A lopsided grin sat on the man's square-jawed face beneath a shock of sun-bleached dirty blonde hair. In black tactical pants, black department polo, and combat boots, he loomed large on the stage. Beside him trotted a mostly black dog.

She swallowed, hoping none of the drool ran out. Damn.

"Carter is accompanied by his partner, Maverick," the emcee said. "For his date, Carter has planned an evening at the zoo for a behind-the-scenes tour of the elephant exhibit. The tour also includes a paint-and-sip event with Thelma the African elephant. The event also includes dinner."

"That sounds like a fun date." Brooke glanced at Mara and grinned.

"What?" Mara's eyes flitted to her friend, then back to the stage. "Oh, yes. You're right, it does."

"One thousand!" Brooke's hand shot up, and she waved her paddle.

"What are you doing?" Mara frowned. She didn't understand why Brooke would bid on anyone. Her friend was happily engaged. They were just here tonight to watch, have fun, and support Gemma.

"Buying you a date."

"What? No." She grabbed Brooke's arm and yanked it down when she would have raised her bid.

"Oh, yes." Brooke wrenched her arm away and raised it. "Fifteen hundred!"

"You cannot spend that kind of money on a date for me. Are you crazy?"

Brooke giggled and held her arm out to the side as Mara made another grab for it. "No. I saw the look on your face when he stepped out. I've never seen you look at a man like that. And, honey, it's past time for you to go on a date. It's been three years since Blake died."

Mara didn't need that reminder. She was well-aware of how long she'd been a widow. "So? There's no timeline on grief."

Brooke raised her paddle. "Eighteen hundred!" She glanced at Mara. "I know, but you're not grieving anymore. Not the way you want people to think. You wouldn't have looked at Deputy Townsend like that if you weren't ready to put yourself out there again. You're just scared." She grinned. "I'm giving you a push."

"Brooke—"

"Twenty-one hundred!" Brooke waved her paddle, hopping on her toes.

"Oh my God." Mara groaned and covered her face. "Would you stop? Please?"

"Do I hear twenty-two?" The emcee's voice carried over the crowd. "Going once..."

"Sweet Jesus," Mara muttered. This wasn't happening.

"Going twice..."

"Someone please bid. Anyone." She peeked through her fingers as she prayed for divine intervention.

Brooke giggled and bounced on the balls of her feet.

"Sold! To number fifty-two for twenty-one hundred dollars." The emcee banged her gavel.

Mara groaned. "I can't believe you did that."

"Believe it, sister. You now have a date for Valentine's Day."

"I hate you so much right now."

The smile on Brooke's face told Mara she didn't care. "You'll thank me one day."

"For setting me up on a blind date with a man you bought at a charity auction?"

Brooke's head bobbed once. "Yep. You watch." She wagged her paddle at Mara. "This will be the start of a new chapter in your life."

"I like the chapter I'm in." It was safe. Nothing could trample on her heart and make it bleed again.

"It's overdone, and you need to start a new one."

The emcee's voice echoed over the crowd, drowning out anything Mara would have said. She flattened her lips together and stared at the stage. There was no arguing with Brooke when she got an idea in her head. It didn't matter what Mara said at this stage. Brooke would still think she was right.

Well, fine. She'd just have to prove her wrong. She'd go on the date with Deputy Townsend, then tell Brooke she tried, but was happy with the status quo. He was sexy, but Mara was happy with her life the way it was. She didn't need a man.

The rest of the auction flew by for Mara. She barely paid attention, lost in her thoughts. When the final bachelor sold and the gavel banged, Brooke grabbed Mara's arm.

"Come on. Let's go meet your date."

Groaning, Mara followed her friend through the surging crowd toward the registration table, where women were lining up to pay for their dates.

"Do you see him?" Brooke stood on her toes, trying to peer over the crowd.

Mara shook her head. "No. There are too many people." She wasn't much taller than Brooke.

"Ladies, let's form a thinner line." The emcee walked up, clapping her hands to get everyone's attention. "Our bachelors are going to come up alongside everyone, so you can meet."

The crowd shifted, snaking out into the arena to accommodate her request. Mara glanced toward the stage and saw the line of men coming out from behind. It wasn't hard to spot Deputy Townsend. Not only was he the most attractive one of the bunch, but he had his K-9 partner at his side. The dog was as beautiful as he was.

Brooke leaned to the side and waved her paddle, a wide smile on her face. "Deputy Townsend."

Mara tried to shrink into the people around her as he walked up, a polite smile on his face.

"Hello."

A shiver went through Mara at the sound of his deep voice, leaving gooseflesh on her arms. It was like butter, but had a bit of gravel to it.

"Hi," Brooke chirped. "I'm Brooke McGinty."

He held out a hand. "Carter Townsend. It's nice to meet you. Thank you for your generosity to the women's crisis center."

"Oh, you're welcome. I was happy to do it." Brooke smiled up at him as she shook his hand. She let go, then stepped back, waving Mara forward.

Mara stood there, arms crossed, and blinked at Brooke, still not happy.

"Deputy, this is my friend Mara Roth. She's your date."

Carter blinked, nonplussed. "Oh." He frowned. "You bid on me for your friend?"

"Yes. I'm happily engaged." Brooke raised her left hand and waggled her fingers, showing off her engagement ring. "But Mara needs to get back out into the dating pool. This seemed like a good opportunity. No pressure or expectations."

He tipped his head, studying Mara. His liquid silver gaze burned into her, turning the gooseflesh to a heated flush.

"Well, it's nice to meet you, Mara." He extended a hand. "I'm sure we'll have a pleasant time."

Oh, God. He wants me to touch him? The feelings he

evoked just standing there were bad enough. With a long blink, she steeled herself and took his hand. It was a brief handshake, but it was enough to send a tingle up her arm that electrified her entire body.

"It's nice to meet you, deputy."

"Call me Carter, please."

She gave him a tight smile and nodded.

The line shuffled forward, and Mara glanced at the dog at his side. "Your dog's name is Maverick, right?"

He nodded.

"What breed is he?" He looked like a German Shepherd, but she wasn't a good judge of dog breeds. Give her horses, though, and she could name it with a quick glance.

"Belgian Malinois."

"He's pretty."

One side of his mouth lifted, and he glanced at the dog, who looked up. "Don't listen to her. You're handsome."

Brooke laughed. Mara felt her lips twitch. "My apologies, Maverick." She unfolded her arms and glanced at Carter. "May I pet him?"

"Sure. He's off duty."

Mara held a hand out to let the dog sniff her, then scratched the side of his face near his ear. His tongue lolled out, and he stared up at her like a puppy.

Carter's rich laugh rolled over her. "You hit the sweet spot. He likes you."

"I'm glad. I wouldn't want to be on his bad side."

"Unless you're on the wrong side of the law—and running away—I think you're safe."

Mara smiled and scratched Maverick's ear again. She straightened, removing her hand, and he stepped forward to nudge her, making her laugh. "I guess I really did hit the sweet spot." She ran her fingers through his soft fur. A smile still on her face, she glanced at Carter. He watched her with a slight furrow between his eyes.

His expression quickly cleared, and he smiled again. "I guess I should probably get your phone number and address." He withdrew his phone from his pocket.

"Right." Mara told him her information. A moment later, her phone vibrated as he texted her his number.

"It was lovely to meet you both. Mara, I'll see you Monday evening. Wear something comfortable. We'll be doing some walking."

Mara's smile turned tight at the reminder of their date. She nodded. "See you then."

He lifted a hand as he backed away. "Have a good evening." Turning, he and Maverick loped toward the exit.

Mara wished she could escape as easily.

Brooke squealed and grabbed her arm. "He's even hotter close up. And that voice." She rolled her eyes and laid a hand over her heart. "If I weren't blissfully happy with Johnathan, I would have bid on him for myself."

"Speaking of, is he going to have a conniption when he finds out you spent over two grand on a date for me?" Mara crossed her arms and lifted an eyebrow.

"It's my money." Brooke waved a hand. "I can do with it as I please. And you know I have plenty to cover the cost."

It was true. Brooke was an event and wedding planner, but she didn't need to work. Her family owned a local luxury resort.

"Besides, you'd do the same for me if I needed the push to put myself back out there." She grinned. "Well, maybe not spend two thousand dollars, but you'd set me up." Brooke waved a finger in Mara's face. "Don't deny it. You know you would."

A smile toyed with Mara's lips. "Maybe." She'd want her friend to be happy. And Brooke was right. If she thought putting herself out there would make her happy, she'd set Brooke up in a heartbeat.

Some of the fight leached out of her. Brooke just wanted her to be the best version of herself. And truthfully, Mara was a bit stuck in the mud. She'd lost herself since she lost her husband. But she wasn't sure she was ready to come out of her protective shell. It just hurt too much when things went sour.

Two

Crisp, wintery air filled Mara's lungs as she stepped into the outdoor arena with her horse, Stinger. The black gelding pawed at the dirt, ready for their morning ride. Dust rose to sparkle in the sunshine. It was a beautiful day.

Mara closed the gate, then mounted Stinger, nudging him into a trot to warm him up. With the bite to the air, she wanted his muscles nice and warmed up before she put him through some runs. He had other ideas, though, and she had to rein him in several times when he tried to work his way into a slow canter. Stinger loved to run.

Once she was sure he was limber enough, she trotted to the gate and turned to face the arena. Three barrels sat arranged in the dirt. Stinger tossed his head and let out a soft whicker. Mara leaned forward and patted his neck. "Let's do this, Stinger." She dug her heels into his sides, and he took off for the first barrel. Mara leaned low as he tore around the barrel and raced across to the next one. Dirt flew as he rounded it, launching them up the straightaway to the third barrel. In moments, they were around it and flying back the way they came.

She sat up and pulled on the reins as they passed the fence post Mara used as a finish line. Stinger snorted and danced in the dirt, wanting to go again.

Clapping drew her attention. She glanced back to see Gemma step up on the gate rails, a wide smile on her face.

"Hey, what are you doing here?" Mara trotted over. Gemma was still on maternity leave.

"I came to say good morning to Jasper." She hooked a thumb toward the building and her horse in his stall. "I didn't see Stinger in his stall, and you weren't inside, so I looked out here. He sure does fly. I'll never get tired of watching the two of you."

Mara grinned and patted Stinger's neck. She might not compete anymore, but she still enjoyed the thrill of racing. "Are you allowed to ride yet?"

Gemma wrinkled her nose. "I could, but things are still a touch sore. It's only been four weeks."

"Well, I'll saddle Jasper sometime today and put him through his paces."

"He'd like that. He's probably getting a little squirrely with only the sedate walks during therapy sessions."

"I've been exercising him. But not as much as he's used to, I'm sure."

"I appreciate it. It sucks not being able to ride." She wagged a finger. "Soon, though. I think I'm going to try later this week. At least get in a short, gentle ride." Gemma crossed her arms over the top rail, and her smile changed. "So. Are you looking forward to your date tonight?"

Mara groaned. "I was trying not to think about it."

Gemma chuckled. "Why? Carter's nice. And nice to look at."

"I know, but—" She broke off and sighed. "I haven't been on a date since Blake died." Her husband's death left a hole in her heart that still wasn't filled in. She didn't think it ever would be.

"You can't spend the rest of your life alone, Mara. You're still young. Would he want you to end up a spinster?"

Mara's lips pursed. That was a question she'd asked herself multiple times this weekend. Every time, the answer was no. Blake would want her to move on. He'd want her to remember him, but he wouldn't want her to stay stuck in the past.

But it was damn hard to take that first step.

She shook her head. "I know he wouldn't, but that doesn't make it any easier."

Gemma's smile turned sympathetic. "Carter's a good guy to break into the dating scene with. He's easy-going and a gentleman."

Mara chuckled. "I just hope he can handle a nervous, slightly awkward thirty-four-year-old widow who was shoved into the frying pan by her two best friends."

"What?" Gemma laid a hand over her heart and feigned a shocked look. "I didn't bid on him. Nor did I tell Brooke to do it."

"No." Mara laughed. "But I'm sure you encouraged her to make me come. You also helped organize the whole thing."

Gemma shrugged. "I'll cop to that. But my goal wasn't to get you a date. It was to get you to have some fun. You work, then go home and bury your nose in a book."

"Hey. I like my book boyfriends."

"I like mine, too, but my husband is a whole lot more satisfying."

Mara's mouth twisted. She did miss sex. Her relationship with Blake had been fun. He wasn't the most spontaneous partner, but she had no complaints about his ability to satisfy her. He knew how to work her into a frenzy and had never left her hanging. Her problem now was getting past the idea that her sexual partner wasn't Blake. She never thought there would be another man in her life. But fate was a cruel bitch and had ripped him away from her.

"Well, regardless, my book boyfriends will have to suffice. I will not be welcoming Carter into my bed tonight." No matter how good he looked.

Her thoughts drifted to the memory of his shoulders and chest outlined by his department polo at the auction, and the dimple that formed in his cheek when he smiled that sexy half-smile of his.

Tendrils of heat started in her belly, spreading outward to her limbs. Mara slammed the door closed on her thoughts. Thinking about him like that would only make her more nervous and tongue-tied tonight.

"Never say never, Mara." Gemma grinned and shook a finger. She hopped off the fence. "I'm headed back in to hang out with my horse. I'll see you later."

Mara swung Stinger away from the fence and waved. "See ya." Her horse danced, ready to run again. She let him, hoping the race chased away her nerves.

THREE

"What do you think, Mav? Am I presentable?" Carter Townsend held out his arms and lifted an eyebrow as he glanced at his dog. The Malinois tilted his head, then barked once.

"That good, huh?" Carter looked in the mirror once more, fixing the hem of his charcoal sweater. He still couldn't believe he was doing this. When he'd agreed to participate, he didn't think much about the actual date portion—the part that came after the auction. Sure, he planned a fun night, but it wasn't until he got out on the stage and saw all the women cheering in the crowd that it hit him he'd have to go out with one of them. Then, the smile on his face turned a little forced, and some sweat popped out on his forehead. He'd kept his feet planted where they were by reminding himself it was for a good cause. They'd turned to lead when he went to meet the winning bidder.

Maverick's easy acceptance of the woman helped ease his mind some. The dog didn't warm up to many people. And Mara seemed nice. It still boggled his mind that her friend would drop that kind of cash on a date for her. Mara must be some friend.

Carter picked up his watch from the dresser and looped it around his wrist. Grabbing his wallet, he headed down the hall. Near the door to the garage, he shoved his feet into a pair of black boots and lifted his shearling-lined gray corduroy coat from the hook. Turning to Maverick, he gave the dog a command, and the animal trotted to his kennel. Carter shut the door on the six-by-six cage and latched it. "I'll be back in a little while, bud."

Maverick spun in a circle on the bed in one corner and laid down with a groan. Carter grinned. His dog was nothing if not dramatic.

Shrugging into his coat, Carter grabbed his keys—and the bouquet of flowers he bought on a whim on his way home— and entered the garage, climbing into his truck. He raised the overhead door and started the vehicle, thankful his house had a garage large enough for the behemoth truck he drove. If there was one thing he hated about living here, it was scraping snow and frost from his windows. Having grown up in Charleston, South Carolina, snow wasn't something he saw much of as a kid. He'd always been envious of the kids who got snow days and could build snowmen. As an adult, though, he couldn't help but wonder what he'd been thinking.

The truck's tires hummed as he drove through town to Mara's house. Foggy Mountain wasn't large, so it was a short drive. The sun's last rays cast a soft glow over her sage-colored house with its white trim. Neat hedgerows lined the front of the house, and she had potted evergreens flanking the porch steps and a white sign with the word "Welcome" painted vertically on it in black block letters. It was inviting and cozy.

Shutting off the truck, Carter grabbed the flowers and got out. On the porch, he pushed the doorbell, listening to it peal inside. Moments later, the heavy wooden door swung inward, and he forgot to breathe. Dressed in jeans and a dark emerald green sweater that contrasted with her coppery red hair, Mara smiled. Her blue eyes crinkled at the corners, telling him it was genuine.

"Hello, deputy." She stepped back. "Come in, please."

Carter cleared his throat, forcing his lungs to work. He brushed past her. "Carter, please."

"Right. Sorry."

"It's okay. I'm nervous too." He held out the flowers. "Here."

"Oh." She took the bouquet of pink roses and brought them to her nose. "They're lovely. You didn't have to do this."

He shrugged. "A woman should get flowers on Valentine's Day."

"Well, thank you." Her smile widened, stealing Carter's breath again. "Walk with me so I can put these in water?" She tipped her head to the rear of the house.

Carter nodded and followed her, glancing around as they passed through the living room and into a short hall. She liked soft colors—grays and creams. Her living room was painted an off-white. Gray furniture clustered around a natural-wood coffee table on a cream rug. The hallway walls were the same color as the living room.

In the kitchen, the colors mirrored the exterior of her home. Her cabinets were a dark sage, the walls the same off-white as the rest of what he'd seen. It all complemented the butcher block counters and black hardware.

She opened a long cupboard in the corner and took a tall crystal vase from inside. Filling it with water, she arranged the flowers in it, then set it on the island. "There. Those look good in here. Thank you again. They're beautiful."

"You're welcome." He offered her a smile. "Are you ready to go? We're supposed to be there by seven."

"Yes. My coat and purse are by the front door." She pointed back the way they'd come.

Carter turned around and led the way to the front of the house. She took a black wool peacoat from the hall tree in the corner and put it on, then picked up her purse from the entryway table.

"All set?" He put a hand on the doorknob.

"Yep."

He opened the door and waved her out, turning the lock before following her outside.

"I didn't take you for a red truck man." She glanced at him as they walked down the short path to the driveway.

Carter lifted an eyebrow. "Why not?" He opened the passenger door.

She shrugged one shoulder and climbed in. "I think maybe it was the all-black outfit you had on at the auction. It made you seem more somber. Are you somber?"

He flashed her a grin. "No." Closing her door, he rounded the hood and got in.

"Not somber, huh?" A smile played with her lips, pulling one from his. "Does that mean you're wild?"

"No," he said with a chuckle. "I'm just a regular guy." He started the truck and backed down the drive and onto the street. "I could ask the same about you. Do you have the personality to match your fiery hair?"

Mara wrinkled her nose, her smile escaping. "My temper can match it sometimes, but that's about all."

Carter nodded once. "So, tell me about yourself. I know a little from Ben and Gemma. You're her boss, right?" he asked, mentioning his boss, Ben Davidson, and the man's wife.

"Yes."

He grinned. "What's that like?" Gemma was great, but she was a firecracker.

Mara laughed. "You know her well."

His chuckle filled the cab alongside hers. "Yeah. She's great, but, man—she'll give you a run for your money."

"She will. She's a hard worker, though. And good at her job. She's a great friend too. I lucked out when I moved here to find a couple of women who I can't imagine life without."

"You're talking about the woman who bid on me? Brooke? That's her name, right?"

Mara nodded. "I'm still aghast she spent that kind of money on me. Which is why I didn't back out last minute."

His brow furrowed slightly as he glanced at her. "Did you want to?"

"Oh, yes. Dating isn't something I do. Did Gemma tell you I was a widow?"

"No. I'm sorry. That must have been rough." He couldn't imagine what that was like. Losing someone you thought you'd grow old with.

"It was. I still miss him, and I think part of me always will." Her voice turned soft, and she looked away.

Carter glanced out his window, his lips tightening. Well, at least he knew where he stood. That should make tonight easier. He could treat her as a friend. They'd have a pleasant time, then part ways.

"Brooke was right, though. I need to put myself back out there."

Or maybe there could be more to this than two friends having a nice evening together. His brows dipped, then smoothed out. Did he want that? He wasn't sure. She was pretty and stirred something in his blood. But he didn't want to be a substitute for a ghost.

"That doesn't mean I'm expecting anything from you." She held her hands up, her eyes going a little wide. "I know the circumstances around our date are a bit—odd. I'm not looking for anything. But I think tonight will be a good test of whether I'm ready to start dating again." She paused for a second, then cocked her head. "That doesn't mean I think you'd make a terrible boyfriend. I'm sure you're a great guy." She stopped, a touch of color highlighting her cheeks.

Carter bit back a smile, amused by the rapid-fire words coming out of her mouth. He glanced over again to see her tuck her bottom lip between her teeth. He chuckled. "I understand what you're saying. I'm not looking to start anything from our date, either. We're fulfilling an obligation." That's what he was going with for now. No expectations.

"Exactly." Her posture relaxed. "I'm glad we're on the same page."

He was too. It would make their time together pass more smoothly if neither of them was looking to get something from this date.

Shifting in his seat, he changed the subject. "So, you said you moved here? How long ago was that?"

"It's been about three years. I took the job as the equestrian center's director just after my husband died. I needed to start over—to get away from the memories."

Running away from bad memories was something Carter could understand. There were plenty of those in his past. "Where are you from, then?"

"Oklahoma. Blake and I lived in Oklahoma City, but I grew up in a small town a couple of hours west of there. We met at my first job in OKC. He was the maintenance director for the facility. After he died, I needed something different."

"I'd say you got your change of scenery."

She smiled. "Yeah. But it helped. I was able to grieve without getting lost in it. Back home, everywhere I looked, something reminded me of him." She glanced at him. "What about you? You're not from the Foggy Mountain area, are you? I think Gemma mentioned something about how happy she was that Ben stole you away from your other department. You met them during the serial killer case, right?"

His mouth slanted up. "Yeah. They saved my mom's life. Our sailboat's engine blew and ripped a hole in the hull. She was trapped below deck and Ben got her out. Maverick too." Carter swallowed hard at the memory. It still hit him like a punch to the gut how close he'd come to losing his mom and his K-9 partner.

Drawing in a deep breath to dispel the disquiet in his mind, he answered the rest of Mara's question. "And Ben didn't exactly steal me. My previous department couldn't afford a K-9 deputy anymore, so Ferris County bought Maverick from them and hired me."

Her eyebrows rose. "Just like that, they bought a dog?"

"It was in their budget already. The dog they had retired and so did his handler, and they hadn't replaced the team yet. I got lucky, I guess. I don't know what would have happened to us otherwise." Thankfully, he hadn't even really needed to worry about it. Ben got wind of the situation and offered to buy the dog almost as soon as Carter was informed they were shutting down his unit.

"Where was this?"

"Fort Carrington. It's south of Asheville."

"Is that where you're from?"

"No. I grew up in Charleston, South Carolina. My mom still lives there."

"How come you aren't there, then? No jobs?"

"Pretty much. I was in the Marines for twelve years. The last four I spent as a dog handler. When I got out, I knew I wanted to continue that, so police work seemed like the most logical step. I spent about a year on patrol—in Charleston— before the opportunity to be a K-9 officer came up. Maverick and I have been partners for almost six years now."

"Why did you leave the Marines? Twelve years is a long time."

"Yeah, well, that's it exactly. It's a long time. And the job I did—it was rough. I needed to leave." He clenched and unclenched his hands around the steering wheel, praying she didn't dig any deeper. It wasn't something he wanted to talk about.

She stared out the window, then at her hands, before glancing at him. "Memories are a bitch."

He let out a soft snort. She had that right. "Yeah."

"I bet your mom's glad to have you closer, though. Is she your only family?"

"I have an aunt there too. My mom's sister. My dad passed away a few years ago from a heart attack. I'm an only child."

"Lucky."

He glanced at her. "To be an only child?"

She nodded. "I have two brothers and a sister. My sister's great, but my brothers are a pain in the ass." She chuckled.

Carter smiled. "Older or younger?"

"Older. Which is why they're a pain in my ass. I'm the youngest. Irish Catholic boys take their duties as big brothers very seriously."

That made him laugh. "I had a guy like that in my unit once. He had a sister in high school who started dating some guy while we were deployed. It drove him nuts that he couldn't be there to interrogate the kid. He finally made her video chat with the boy and grilled him then."

Mara giggled. "Yeah, that sounds like something my brothers would do. Which is why I'm not mentioning this date to them. They'd demand to know everything about you, even though this is just a night out between new friends." She shook her head. "You'd think I was still sixteen instead of thirty-four."

"It's nice that they look out for you, though."

"Yeah, I guess. I love them, but I'm glad they gave me some space when I came here. The silence helped me deal, you know?"

He nodded. He did know. Sometimes, the best way to sort things out was to be alone.

"So, you know how old I am. How old are you?" She shifted in her seat, turning to face him. "I'm guessing mid-thirties, from what you've said."

His head bobbed. "I'll be thirty-seven next month. I entered the Marines right out of high school. What about you? College?"

"Yeah. I was a psychology major. I wanted to be a therapist. The plan was to get a doctorate and open my own practice. Then my university started an equestrian therapy program. That was all she wrote for me. I've been riding since I was a little girl, and the premise of the therapy intrigued me. I wouldn't want to do anything else now."

"Do you still do sessions?"

"Not as much as I'd like. But I like training people how to do it. I find that almost as rewarding. Especially when they go out and spread the knowledge by starting new programs."

"I have a confession." He paused and cast a glance at her from the corner of his eye. "I've never been on a horse."

"Hm, we might have to fix that." She smiled. "I can't believe Gemma hasn't gotten you on one, though. She and Ben go riding a lot."

"She's tried a few times, but something's always come up." He lifted one shoulder and adjusted his grip on the steering wheel. "I figure it'll happen at some point." He glanced at her. "So, did you grow up on a farm or something? You said you've been riding since you were a kid."

"My family owns a small ranch, so I grew up in the saddle. I was actually a champion barrel racer for several years. My winnings bought my first car and made up a decent chunk of the down payment on the house Blake and I bought after we got married."

"Nice. Do you still race?"

"No. I've kept up my skills, but I don't do competitions anymore. It's not really something you can just do on the weekends. It involves traveling a lot. When I was on the youth circuit, the competitions were regional, but on the adult side, they're all over the midwestern and mountain states. It's more of a lifestyle at that point."

"Why psychology and not barrel racing?"

"Because I was smart enough to understand that barrel racing would only last as long as my horse. Sure, my skill played a role, but if you didn't have a fast horse, you weren't going to win. Cultivating that kind of animal takes time and money. At that point, it becomes a business more than a sport. That's not what I wanted."

"Okay, so why psychology?"

She shrugged. "People are interesting."

Carter raised an eyebrow. "That's it? People are interesting?"

She giggled. "That's what sparked my interest, yes. I wanted to learn more about why people are the way they are. Then in college, it turned into wanting to help people figure out why they are the way they are and to help them cope with their problems."

"I've heard good things about equestrian therapy—before I met Gemma. I know a couple guys who've tried it for PTSD."

"Did it help them?"

He nodded. "They're still messed up, but they can function now."

"Soldiers are the hardest to work with. What they—you've—seen—" She broke off and shook her head. "I can't even imagine it."

Carter's muscles tensed again as she treaded into dangerous territory. That was a part of his mind he never went to. Not anymore. "Yeah. It wasn't pleasant." He kept his eyes on the road, praying she'd pick up on his body language and change the subject.

Several beats of silence passed.

"So, tell me more about this event we're going to. The elephant actually paints?"

He let out a slow breath. Thankful she hadn't pressed him for more details about his time in the Marines, the tension left his body. "From what I've heard, yes. It should be interesting."

Their conversation turned to lighter topics as they discussed Thelma, the elephant artist, and the other zoo animals. Neither of them had ever been to the zoo here, so it would be a new experience for them both.

The remainder of the drive passed quickly, and Carter was surprised when the sign for the zoo exit appeared. He'd hoped he and Mara would get along well, so this date wasn't a disaster, but he hadn't anticipated that she'd be so easy to talk to. Or that they would get so absorbed in their conversation.

Following the signs, they soon turned off into the zoo's parking lot. Special event markers guided him to the parking area, and he pulled his truck into a space. The two of them climbed out and made their way to the entrance. Carter showed the attendant their tickets, and the young man waved them through, pointing to the gift shop to their right where everyone was gathering. Another attendant greeted them with a smile and handed them a program.

Carter opened it and held it where Mara could see it. The pamphlet had an itinerary and some information on Thelma and her paintings.

"Looks like dinner's first. Good. I'm hungry."

So was he. Though her soft floral perfume was raising a different hunger. Shifting to put a little distance between them and restore his equilibrium, Carter offered her the program. She waved a hand, so he folded it and tucked it into his back pocket. "This is a smaller event than I thought it would be."

He glanced at the small crowd. There were maybe two dozen people present.

"They probably only have so much space in the area where Thelma paints."

"True." His eyes traveled over the crowd once more, assessing the couples. Some had struck up conversations with other attendees while the rest were in conversation with each other.

The door opened, and another couple came in, followed by a woman in khaki pants and a purple polo. She paused at the fringe of the group and clapped her hands.

"Everyone, may I have your attention, please?"

The room quieted, and all eyes turned to her.

"Welcome to our Valentine's Paint-and-Pour Plus. My name is Alyssa, and I'll be your host this evening. Everyone's here, so we're going to get started. If you'll all follow me?" She turned toward the door and beckoned them to follow.

They all filed out of the gift shop and down the main concourse. As they walked, Alyssa gave them the tour guide spiel about the zoo and its inhabitants. It was hard to see much since it was dark, but what Carter could see looked well-kept.

When they reached the education center, Alyssa led them inside and directed them down the hallway, where she let them into a large auditorium.

"Each table has a place card, so find yours and have a seat. Dinner will be out soon."

Carter laid a hand on Mara's back and ushered her deeper into the room. They wandered through the tables until they found one with his last name and sat down. Their table was in the middle of the room, which bothered him. He didn't like not being able to see the entire room.

His knee bounced as he glanced around, taking note of the exits and the location of the other diners and staff.

"Are you okay?"

He turned around at the sound of Mara's soft question. "Sorry, what?"

"I asked if you were okay. You seem edgy all of a sudden."

Carter forced his shoulders to relax. "Yeah. Sorry. I don't like sitting in the middle of a room. I can't see everything. It's the soldier—and cop—in me. It makes me nervous, but I'll be fine."

"Are you sure?"

He nodded. It was only for a little while, and the idea of trouble here was minimal. "Yes."

Footsteps alerted him to someone coming up from behind. He glanced back to see a server headed for them with a bottle of wine in her hands.

"Hello. Would you like some wine? This is a merlot, but one of my colleagues has a sharp pinot grigio, if you'd prefer that."

Mara raised her glass. "Merlot is fine with me."

Carter nodded and picked up his wine goblet. He preferred red as well.

The lights on the stage came on, and a moment later, a man in a suit came out of the wings and walked to the podium. Carter tuned him out as he thanked everyone for coming and espoused the zoo's outreach program, which events like this one funded. Instead, he crowd-watched.

"So, do you suppose Thelma prefers warm colors or cool colors?"

It took a moment for her question to register. When it did, he looked at her, then grinned at the teasing light in her eyes. "Sorry. I'm not trying to ignore you. And I don't know about Thelma, but I like cool colors."

Her smile bloomed. "I wasn't trying to make you feel guilty. Just trying to distract you."

"You don't need silly quips to do that." The words were

out of his mouth before he thought them through. He didn't take them back, though. They were true. Mara Roth was a beautiful woman.

The crowd faded into background noise as something in his head shifted, giving her his full attention. It was the least she deserved. Real date or not, his behavior was rude. His mom would slap him if she saw him ignoring his companion in favor of satisfying his need for control. He vowed to do better.

Four

Mara's cheeks flushed, and she glanced down, surprised by her reaction to his words. Why, she didn't know. She knew she was no slouch in the looks department, but for whatever reason, hearing Carter admit she distracted him turned her into a heap of flustered woman. She looked at him through her lashes. "That's nice of you to say. Thank you."

He wasn't the only one distracted by the other person. She'd forced her knees not to buckle when she opened the door earlier. He'd been something to look at in his uniform at the auction. But in street clothes? Damn...

Her fingers nudged the linen napkin on the table. She curled them into a fist to keep from picking it up and fanning herself with it. That jacket he had on did something for his shoulders. They looked a mile wide. And it brought a ruggedness to him that she found sexy and appealing. He reminded her of the cowboys back home. She loved a good cowboy.

A round of applause went through the crowd as the speaker finished his presentation. Mara clapped to be polite, but she'd heard nothing the man said. Hopefully, there hadn't been any instructions for later.

The double doors near the stage swung open and a small army of servers flowed out, each carrying a large tray laden with plates. She was happy to see them, and not just because they had food. It gave her a chance to gather herself after the heated tension Carter's words provoked.

They dug into their meals—which were excellent—negating the need to talk for several minutes. Once they'd assuaged their hunger some, their conversation started again, but ranged over light topics. Mara learned more about some of his likes and dislikes, and revealed some of her own.

When dinner was over, Alyssa came back and ushered them all back outside and down the concourse to the elephant enclosure. She led them to the staff entrance and through a set of short hallways to the indoor pens. The sounds made by the big animals reached Mara's ears before she saw them. Several short trumpets met their group as they went through the doorway to the stalls. Then she saw them. One elephant was off by itself in a stall with a heavy white sheet attached to the wall. In another pen, two other elephants watched. Behind them, the door was open to the outside. Heaters blasted overhead, but Mara still shivered. The breeze coming in was chilly.

"Everyone, find an easel." Alyssa motioned to the double line of easels set up in the open area in front of the stalls.

Carter led her to a set of easels in the far corner.

"Is this okay?" He gestured to their spot.

She nodded. "It's fine." The room was small, so any of the easels offered a decent vantage point to watch Thelma create her masterpiece.

When everyone was settled, Alyssa introduced the elephant, as well as the trainer working with her. Mara watched, fascinated, as Thelma picked up a brush with her trunk and dipped it into a can of paint, then swirled it over the sheet hanging on the wall. To her astonishment, the animal drew several shapes.

"How do they get her to do that?" Carter wondered aloud. He looked at Mara. "Do you know?"

She shook her head, just as amazed as he was. They weren't the only ones wondering, though. A woman in the front asked Alyssa that question.

"That's a very good question. Thelma's trainers are always in search of activities to keep her and the other elephants engaged. One of them saw a video on the internet of an elephant painting and decided to try it with a few of ours. Thelma loved it and would mimic shapes and lines her trainers drew. Now, she paints almost every day—at her discretion. If she's not interested, the trainers don't push. Her artwork has helped fund improvements to the elephant enclosure here at the zoo, as well as enrichment activities for her herd."

The trainer in with Thelma stepped forward, but stayed in the pen with her. "We've been working with Thelma to paint scenery. As you can see, she's working on a forest." The woman motioned to the trees taking shape on the canvas. "You all are going to paint your version of a forest on the canvases we've had her mark with her signature. When you're done, you'll all have your own piece of elephant art."

"I'm not sure I thought this through," Carter muttered, leaning toward her.

Mara gave him a curious frown. "What do you mean?"

"What am I going to do with this?" He gestured to the canvas on his easel with its blue trunk/nose print in the lower righthand corner.

Mara giggled. "Hang it in your house." She was planning to give hers to one of her nieces. Desi loved elephants and would love the piece.

He rolled his eyes. "It'll go so well with my décor."

She chuckled. "You could always try to sell it. Or donate it."

Carter sighed and picked up a paintbrush. "I'll figure something out. What are you going to do with yours?"

"Give it to my niece. She'll think it's cool."

"Does she want two?" He dipped his brush in the brown paint.

"She has a sister. I can ask."

His head bobbed. "Do that. I hope they're really young and not picky." He smeared brown paint on the canvas, making a tree trunk. "A masterpiece this won't be."

"They're four and two, so you're good."

A quick laugh burst free of his chest. "Good."

Giggling softly, Mara dipped her paintbrush in the brown paint and started on her own tree trunks. She actually quite liked to draw, so she had high hopes for her painting. Tongue poking between her teeth, she concentrated on her art. Once she had the trunks painted, she grabbed the green to start on the foliage. Cleaning off her brush, she glanced at Carter's canvas and couldn't hold back the chuckle.

"Don't laugh. I know it's terrible. I never claimed to be an artist." He dabbed some green on top of a branch.

Her laughter increased. "It's not that bad."

"Liar."

"Addie will love it."

"Yeah, because it'll look like something she did."

Mara let out a snort, then covered her mouth, her cheeks turning red. She laughed harder, and Carter joined her.

"Oh, that's funny." She wiped her eyes.

He grinned and added a bird to his painting with a swish of black. "You think I can paint an elephant?"

Mara snorted again. She'd like to see him try.

His smile widened, and he reached for the white, mixing it with some black.

Fifteen minutes later, he had several gray blobs on top of poles, with long appendages coming off their fronts. Mara, though, had added shading to her trees and outlined her elephants.

"We're definitely giving mine to the two-year-old. She'll be less likely to protest." Carter eyed her work.

Mara giggled and started painting in her animals.

Over the next thirty minutes, they talked as they worked, laughing and enjoying their evening. Mara was surprised at how relaxed she was. She'd expected things to be more awkward—like most first dates she'd been on. But Carter was quick-witted and easy to talk to. All too soon, they were putting their paints away and leaving the elephant enclosure with their semi-dry paintings.

Their tour director, Alyssa, led them through the zoo to the front entrance and thanked them all for coming. Mara preceded Carter through the gate and headed for his truck.

They deposited their paintings on the backseat, then got in. Mara rubbed her hands together and bounced her knees, trying to chase away the chill. Carter cranked on the heat before pulling out of his space.

"So, tell me more about these nieces of yours," he said once they were on the highway headed north. "Which sibling do they belong to?"

"My middle brother, Jameson. He's got the two girls, Desiree—Desi—and Addie. He has an infant son, too—George." She missed those kids, even though she saw them at Christmas. At their age, they changed so fast. Every time she video-chatted with them, the girls both looked like they'd grown an inch, and George had figured out some new thing that made him even cuter.

"Do you have other nieces or nephews?"

"My older brother, Kiernan, has two sons—Miles and Beckett. They're eleven and nine. My sister, Hannah, has one of each—Cassidy and Keegan. They're the same ages as Kiernan's kids."

"I bet it's a lot of fun at Christmas."

She nodded. "It's very loud."

He chuckled. "I bet. I always wanted siblings, but my parents had trouble having kids. I spent a lot of time with my cousins, though, growing up. We don't see each other as much now as I'd like, but it was nice when we were young."

"I'm glad. I can't imagine what it's like to not have that bond. My brothers drive me crazy, but it would be weird without them. And I talk to my sister almost every day."

Carter shrugged. "You get used to being alone, I guess. I still talk to my cousins, but we don't get together much. Over the holidays when we can. I went home for Thanksgiving this past year, but had to work Christmas and New Year's. I'm hoping to go back for Easter, though."

"I was home for Christmas. It was great. I got my dose of baby snuggles." Her heart ached for what would likely never be for her. It was hard to be around her siblings and their families sometimes, but she would never avoid them to save herself the reminder of the future she'd lost when Blake died. Seeing the kids' delighted smiles and hearing their belly laughs soothed something in her soul.

"No babies for you?"

She frowned. "I'm a widow, remember?"

He shrugged. "That doesn't mean you can't remarry. Or have a baby on your own. Or adopt."

"I wouldn't want to raise a child by myself. It's hard enough with two people. As for remarrying—I don't know. Blake was supposed to be it for me. I guess maybe if the right man came along, I would." She cast a glance at Carter through her lashes, watching him as he drove. Her words rang in her head, and she couldn't help but wonder if this was the start of something that could lead her back to that. He'd certainly piqued her interest.

She slammed the door on those thoughts. There were no

expectations with tonight's date. None. This wasn't supposed to turn into anything. She shouldn't even be entertaining those thoughts.

And yet, she wanted to know more about him. Wanted to see him again.

Mara turned and looked out the window, glad it was dark so he couldn't see the thoughts on her face. What a mess she'd gotten herself into.

FIVE

Carter pulled his truck into Mara's driveway and put it in park, reluctant to end their evening. This had been a much more delightful experience than he'd anticipated. Mara was smart and funny, talented, and easy-going. They'd talked almost non-stop all night. He couldn't remember a better first date.

Not that this was a date. They'd agreed they were just fulfilling the obligation of the auction—nothing more.

So, why did he wish it were more?

The interior light lit up as Mara opened her door. "Thanks for a wonderful evening, Carter. I had a nice time."

"So did I." He glanced over the seat at their artwork. "Let me help you with those." He shut the truck off and opened his door, climbing out. Opening the rear door, he removed his painting. Mara grabbed hers, then he followed her to the front door.

She rooted in her purse for her keys, quickly finding them and letting them inside.

"Let's set them on the dining table. They still need to dry."

She led him deeper into the house to the table in the far corner of the kitchen.

"Tell your brother I'm sorry for the eyesore about to be hung in his house."

Mara laughed. "It'll go in her room, most likely, so the only person who'll have to look at it regularly will be Addie."

"Good. Though, I'm not sure that's the best place. It might give her nightmares and scar her for life." He glanced at the painting. It really was a sorry sight. Mara should paint over it—preserving Thelma's signature—and give her niece a better piece of art.

She lightly smacked his arm, smiling. "Stop it. You tried your best."

He grinned. "I know. And it was fun." His smile faded as he stared at her. "I'm glad your friend bid on me for you. I had a good time." He still didn't want it to end, but he really didn't have a reason to linger. He glanced away. "Well, I guess I should be going." Carter took a step back, but her hand on his arm made him pause.

"Wait. Would you like a cup of coffee before you go?"

"Coffee?"

She nodded, a blush staining her cheeks. "Yes. Or water. Or you could even have another glass of wine and stay awhile."

The desire to do just that punched him in the gut. He could easily see himself staying all night. For more than a glass of wine. He swayed a step closer, eyes roving over her face to pause on her pouty, pink lips. The lance of fire that went straight to his groin sent common sense rolling back in. This was a bad idea. He'd never been the type to sleep with a woman on their first date. He'd never even had a one-night stand. Mara would not be the first.

But that didn't mean he wanted to leave just yet. "How about some coffee? I have to work tomorrow, so I can't stay too late."

A flash of something flitted through her eyes—disappointment?—but then she smiled and anything he thought he saw disappeared.

"Me too." She let out a soft giggle, turning toward the counter. "Coffee's probably not the best idea for either of us." She paused, glancing back. "What about some cookies and milk?"

He was about to tell her that sounded great when she laughed.

"God, listen to me. I sound like my grandma when she used to ask us if we wanted cookies and milk when we came to her house as kids." Her cheeks flushed to match her hair, which Carter found adorable. Mara's wholesomeness was wonderful. "I don't think you're a kid, though. Not at all."

Carter's blood heated as her eyes roved over his body. He fought to keep his eyes on her face and not do the same. "There's nothing wrong with emulating your elders. And I'll always take cookies. What kind?"

Some of her embarrassment faded, and she relaxed a bit. "Snickerdoodles. I love cinnamon."

"Me too. Those are my favorite cookie."

She turned around, heading for the counter again, but glanced back. "Really? Most people say chocolate chip."

"Yep. I like chocolate, but I'll almost always choose a snickerdoodle if given a choice. Or oatmeal raisin."

He followed her deeper into the kitchen and helped her pour two glasses of milk and put cookies on a plate.

"Do you want to go in the living room, or would you rather stay in here?" Mara asked.

"Whichever you prefer. The living room is probably more comfortable, though, right?"

"Infinitely." She picked up the cookie plate and her glass of milk. "Come on." She led him down the short hallway to her light and bright living room.

Carter waited for her to pick a seat, then sat down on the other end of the couch. He picked up a cookie off the plate she set down and took a bite. Cinnamon exploded over his tongue. "Mmm." He swallowed the bite. "This is really good."

"Thanks. It's my grandma's recipe."

His eyebrow shot up. "You made these?"

She nodded.

"What do I have to do to get these more often?"

Her cheeks flushed, and he realized how his words sounded. Heat suffused his face, and he chuckled. "I did not mean that how it sounded." He stuffed the rest of the cookie in his mouth and glanced away. *Great job, idiot. Way to put your foot in your mouth.* His inner voice rolled its eyes at him. He wouldn't mind another date, but the implication he wanted to see her again could have been smoother.

Mara waved a hand. "I know."

"I wouldn't be opposed to another date ending like this one, though." He reached for another cookie as he threw that out there. Part of him wanted to take it back. He had no desire for a relationship; too much about his past was too painful to discuss. And he knew that for a relationship to work, he had to be open about the things he'd done and seen—which he wasn't ready for. But he'd be damned if something about her didn't override the part of him that wanted to stay hidden behind walls.

She froze, cookie between her teeth. After a moment, she bit off a bite and chewed it up. "You wouldn't?"

"No. I know we agreed this wasn't a date, but Mara, I've never had a better date. Tonight was fun. Not just because of where we went, but because I was with you. Would you like to go out again? This time for real?" Carter was glad his hands were busy. He wasn't a naturally nervous man, but right now he was. Despite his misgivings about what it would mean for his emotional state, he wanted her to say yes. Watching her while she stared off into the distance, contemplating his question, was torture.

"Um, actually, I think that sounds great. I had a nice time, too, Carter."

Elation and relief put a wide smile on his face. "Good. Great. This weekend, maybe?"

She nodded.

"Great." Geez, he sounded like a damn parrot. He took another bite of his cookie and shut up.

Six

A soft knock sounded on Mara's door. She glanced up from her computer screen to see Gemma standing in the doorway.

"Hey." She smiled at her friend. "Back to exercise Jasper?"

Gemma returned her smile. "Yeah. I'm going to give a slow walk a go. It's killing me to not ride. I also wanted to see if you'd like to get lunch."

"Oh. Sure." Lunch with Gemma sounded much better than the soup and sandwich she packed.

"Great. Give me about forty-five minutes?"

"That's perfect. I have a report to finish."

"Awesome. See you in a bit."

Mara nodded, and Gemma disappeared, her riding boots making soft thuds as she moved down the hallway to go to the stables.

Turning back to her screen, Mara returned to her report. Forty minutes later, she logged out. Grabbing her purse and jacket, she left her office and told the office manager, Pam, where she was going, then headed for the stables to find Gemma.

Soft neighs met her presence as she walked down the corridor to Jasper's stall.

Gemma glanced up and smiled. "Hey, I'm about done."

"Take your time. I don't really have anything pressing this afternoon until two. Did you have a good ride?"

"Yes. It wasn't too bad. I'm definitely not ready for more than a walk, but I can work with that. It was nice to have a distraction and something to perk me up."

"Oh? Meri keeping you up at night?" Gemma's daughter, Meredith, was only a few weeks old.

"That's part of it, but mostly it's a case Ben's working."

"A case? Since when do his cases bother you?"

"Since it involves our friend's girlfriend."

"What?" Mara's eyebrows dipped, confused.

"Let me finish dressing Jasper down. We can talk about it over lunch. I want to hear about your date with Carter too."

Mara rolled her lips in and nodded. She should have known that topic would come up. It was too late to turn down lunch, though. She would not be rude to avoid talking about her personal life. Especially to someone who had helped her reconstruct the pieces of her shattered life with zero questions asked. Plus, it would be nice to get someone else's take on what was happening with Carter. She'd kept the news of her date from her sister on the several occasions they'd talked this past week. It wasn't that she didn't want Shauna to know. She just didn't want her brothers to know. Not yet. Shauna was not the best at keeping secrets. Her mouth frequently ran ahead of her brain, and things just slipped out.

Gemma paused, the brush in her hand hovering over Jasper's back. "Oh, I like that look." She pointed at Mara's face with the brush.

"What look?" Mara wasn't aware she had a look other than one of resignation.

"The one that says you had a good time and want to do it

again." She resumed her task of sweeping dust off the horse's back. "Do tell."

All that had been on her face? She let out a short breath. "I will. Over lunch." She grinned at her friend, her expression lightening as she reminded Gemma of her earlier statement about waiting to talk.

Gemma's quick laugh filled the stall. "Touché."

Giggling, Mara picked up Jasper's saddle and saddle blanket and headed for the tack room.

With Jasper settled, Mara and Gemma left the building through the arena and got into Gemma's car.

"Where to?" Gemma started the engine.

"I don't care. What do you want?"

"Chinese?"

"Sure."

Gemma put the car in gear and backed out of her parking space, then pointed them toward Foggy Mountain's only Chinese restaurant. Once there, they found a space near the rear of the lot and went inside.

"We should have waited another hour. I forgot about the lunch rush." Gemma brushed her hair back into place as the door closed behind them, cutting off the wind.

"I think we'll be fine. I see some empty tables."

The hostess arrived just then and showed them to a table in the middle of the restaurant. They quickly placed their orders, both knowing what they liked.

"So." Gemma folded her hands on the table and leaned forward. "Tell me about your date."

"We had a good time. Better than I ever thought we would. I was so nervous, but it didn't take me long to relax. He's kind and funny. We never lacked for conversation."

"That's great. So, do you feel ready to reenter the dating world now?"

A grin stole over Mara's face. "Actually, he asked if I'd like to go out again. I said yes. We're having dinner tomorrow evening. He offered to cook for me."

Gemma gasped. "What? That's great. I'd hoped you'd hit it off with Carter—he's such a great guy—but I knew you were just breaking into dating again, so I didn't want to get my hopes up. I'm glad things went well."

"Me too. Brooke did well picking my date." Mara chuckled. "Carter's very easy-going, which helped. I didn't feel pressured into making small talk or all the things that go into a first date. We agreed at the beginning it wasn't a date. Just two people going out for an evening as friends. By the end of the night, I didn't want him to go home. We ended up at my house and just talked for about an hour before he needed to leave." She'd thought she was going to get a kiss, which she did —on the cheek. It still set her on fire, though, and made her eager for their next date.

"Well, good. It sounds like he makes you happy."

"He does. I never imagined I'd feel like this again. I just hope I don't get my heart broken."

"Carter's a good guy. If things don't work between the two of you, I think it'll be a mutual thing. He won't string you along."

"That doesn't mean it won't still hurt if it ends." Mara had battled that thought all week. Several times, she'd almost called him and canceled. But then she remembered Gemma's words about how Blake wouldn't want her to live her life alone, and she pushed the thought away for a little while again.

"No, but at least you'll know you tried."

Their server arrived with their drinks. Mara took the opportunity to change the subject once the girl walked away.

"So, what's going on with the sheriff's department that's causing you to lose sleep?" She unwrapped her straw and stuck it in her drink.

Gemma's forehead pinched. "Do you remember Cullen

Tate? The county coroner? He was in the news during the Derek Sutton case when I was kidnapped."

Mara nodded. She'd never met the man, but she knew he was a friend of Gemma's and Ben's.

"So that bombing at the hospital in Asheville was his girlfriend's car. Something's going on with their pharmacy. Ben mentioned a drug cartel—the ATF and DEA are involved. It's a mess. What's got me upset is Piper—Cullen's girlfriend—was kidnapped yesterday."

Mara gasped. "Oh my goodness! That's awful. Does Ben have any leads?"

"Nothing that's panning out. They're not even sure who all is involved other than a couple of pharmacy employees—who no one can locate now." She ran a hand through her hair, then picked up her straw and ripped the paper off.

"How's Cullen?"

"Stoic, as ever. But he's hurting. Ben said he had to convince him to go home last night. He ended up at his office working all night. And he went to the hospital this morning to work. I called him to see if he needed anything, and I could hear a page go off in the background. He said he's trying to stay busy, so he doesn't dwell on what could be."

Mara let out a soft snort. "I get that. When Blake died, I buried myself in work. Nights were the worst. I couldn't get away from it then."

"Yeah. I just hope they find her soon. One way or another. Cullen's a very reserved man. He doesn't let many people in, and he doesn't wear his heart on his sleeve. What's going on with Piper has to be tearing him apart." Gemma glanced away and took a deep breath before looking at Mara again. "Anyway, that's what's going on with me. The ride helped me clear my head some. Thank you for listening to me vent."

"Of course. I'm glad I was free." Her friendship with Gemma was one Mara dearly valued. She and Brooke had been a lifeline as she grieved her husband. Anytime she could lend an ear, she was happy to do so. "If there's anything I can do, let me know."

"I will." Gemma shoved her straw into her drink. "Can we talk about something else? I need a distraction."

"Sure. Tell me about your baby. She do anything fun since I saw you last?"

Instantly, Gemma's face brightened at the mention of her daughter. A soft smile curved her mouth. "She smiled. I had one of her crinkly rattles and was waving it over her face. She reached a hand up for it and smiled. We can already see bits of her personality coming out. She's going to be a lot like me, I'm afraid. She's very demanding."

Mara laughed. "Poor Ben."

Gemma giggled. "Poor Ben, nothing. He knew what he was getting into when he married me."

"Still—I'm betting he hopes the next kid is a boy."

"Probably." Laughing, she took a drink of her water.

Mara grinned and shook her head. She wasn't sure a boy would be any different. Something told Mara any baby Gemma had would end up being a handful.

A pang of melancholy set off an ache in Mara's heart. Once upon a time, she imagined she'd be where Gemma was now. Happily married with a baby. But that dream died with Blake.

Carter's face flashed in her mind.

Or so she thought. Maybe the dream wasn't dead.

Whether it was or not, she was a long way off from a child of her own. And it would do her well to remember that just because she was putting herself out there again, didn't mean she could resurrect a future she'd buried. Life didn't work that way.

SEVEN

Mara put her car in park in Carter's driveway and eyed the single-story structure through her windshield. The small brick ranch was tidy, but plain. No plants or decorations adorned his porch. Evergreen hedges lined the flowerbeds that were in need of some mulch and edging. Maybe this spring, if they were still together, he'd let her get her hands on it and spruce it up a bit. It had a lot of potential.

Exiting her car, she locked it and slid the keys into her purse as she walked up the two steps to the porch and rang the bell. She heard toenails on wood, then heavier footfalls near the door and the muffled sound of Carter's voice a moment before the door opened.

"Hi." He smiled. "Come in." Stepping back, he motioned her inside.

Mara stepped over the threshold and glanced around. The front door opened into a small entryway. To the left was a small living room. Brown leather furniture faced an entertainment center that boasted a large television. A few art prints adorned the other walls, making the room feel less stark. It was still empty compared to her house, though. Why didn't men ever want to decorate? Or at least the ones she knew? What was wrong with some color and comfort in a house?

"Let me take your coat."

She shrugged out of it and handed it to him. "Thanks."

With a nod, he opened a coat closet and put it on a hanger and hung it on the bar inside. When he turned back, she noticed his expression looked pinched.

"Are you all right?"

Carter nodded. "Yeah. I'm just tired. It was a long night, and I didn't get much sleep when I got home. Too keyed up."

A wrinkle marred the space between Mara's eyes. "What happened?"

"We found Piper Riordan. She was near death from hypothermia."

Mara inhaled a sharp breath.

"I talked to Ben a little while ago, and she's going to be fine."

"That's great. I know Gemma was worried yesterday. About her and about Cullen Tate."

"Yeah. He was a mess last night. Until we found her. Then he showed us why he's a leader in his field."

Mara frowned. "As a coroner?"

Carter shook his head. "No. He's a trauma surgeon. He took charge and had Piper packaged and ready to go to the hospital in minutes. The coroner thing is in addition to his other duties."

"Oh." She hadn't known that.

A soft whine from the corner drew her attention. She glanced over to see Maverick sitting in a large dog kennel, the door open.

Carter called the dog over and had him sit. Maverick raised a foot and whined.

Mara laughed. "Hi, buddy."

Rolling his eyes, Carter released the dog from his hold, and the animal scooted toward Mara, working his head under her hand. Mara scratched his ears.

"I still don't understand it."

She glanced up to see him watching them, shaking his head.

"He likes very few people well enough to seek out attention. Even with me, it took a couple of weeks before he'd come find me and want to be pet."

Mara shrugged, continuing to pet the dog. "Animals are like people in some ways. There are certain people who just click with them. We have a few horses I can't put with certain riders because it makes the animal skittish. Those same horses will nudge other riders for head scratches."

He let out a soft grunt. "I hope you're prepared to have a dog if something happens to me. He's picked you, and I'll be sure to let Ben know."

She gave him a curious frown. "Wouldn't they pair him with another handler?"

Carter shook his head. "Not with our history and his age. By the time he got used to another handler—if he did—he'd be at or close to retirement."

"Oh, well, in that case, I'd be happy to take him. Though I hope it never comes to that."

"You and me both." He tipped his head toward the rear of the house. "Come on. I've got the main part of our dinner in the oven, but I'm still working on the sides."

Mara smiled and followed him. Maverick trotted along behind them. "What did you make?"

"Shrimp tacos."

"In the oven?" She'd never heard of it being done that way.

"Just the shrimp."

"Oh. I've never cooked shrimp in the oven."

"I do it all the time. It's good with smoked sausage and peppers too."

That did sound good. She'd have to remember that. And find out how long and at what temp to cook them. "So, what do you want me to do?" She set her purse on the floor out of the way and glanced around the kitchen, taking in the natural-wood cabinets, white walls, and gray-flecked granite counters. He had several items piled on the center island.

"Just sit and talk to me. I'm making slaw to top the tacos. And the rice is about done."

"Okay." She perched on a stool at the end of the island to watch him work. It was nice to get a home-cooked meal she didn't have to make. That only ever happened when she went home to Oklahoma. Even when she was married, it didn't happen often. Blake didn't really like to cook.

Easy conversation flowed between them while Carter finished dinner and they ate. Topics ranged from her work at the equestrian center to some of the crazier calls Carter and Maverick had attended. Like their first evening together, Mara felt comfortable in his presence. Even more so than before.

"I'm full. That was wonderful." Mara smiled as she stood to take her plate to the dishwasher.

"I'm glad you liked it. Next time, I'll have to make that shrimp and sausage stuff."

She waved a finger at him as she straightened from depositing her dish in the rack. "Next time, it's my turn."

He nodded once, bringing his plate over. Bending, he put it in the rack, then closed the door and stepped closer. "Deal."

Mara swallowed, her throat suddenly dry at his nearness. She watched as his silvery eyes turned a stormy color. He dipped his head.

A car alarm blared outside. Maverick woofed from his spot on the floor. Carter straightened and turned toward the sound, a frown wiping out the desire on his face.

Letting out a soft huff of disappointment that she hadn't

gotten to taste his sculpted lips, she blinked. The closeness of the sound registered. "That sounds like it's right outside."

"Yeah." Turning away, he walked out of the kitchen, calling Maverick. The dog got up and trotted after his handler, ears up, posture alert.

Mara trailed behind them, wanting to know what was going on, but not wanting to get in the way. They reached the front window, and Mara gasped as she saw her car lights flashing.

Carter looked at her, his expression all cop. "Where are your keys?"

"In my purse." She motioned back the way they'd come.

"Go get them."

She scurried to the kitchen and retrieved her purse, digging through it as she returned to the living room. The keys jingled as she pulled them out.

Carter took them and headed for the front door. "It's probably nothing, but stay inside."

Mara nodded, her heartbeat a little quicker than usual. She had no problem staying in here and letting him take care of things.

"Maverick, *fuss.*"

If possible, the dog's posture turned even more alert as he followed Carter out the door. He looked like a coiled spring, ready to burst free.

Chewing on the corner of her bottom lip, Mara stood in the doorway and watched as the two of them approached her vehicle. Carter silenced the alarm, then walked around the car. He jogged to the end of the drive, looking both ways on the road, then turned around and came back to the house. She stepped back to let him and Maverick inside.

"Well?" She closed the door behind them.

"Someone broke the rear window out of your car." He took his phone from his pocket.

"What?" Her eyebrows slammed down, and she glanced toward the door.

"I'm calling it in."

Mara covered her mouth with her hands and shook her head. Why would someone break her window?

EIGHT

Whistling, Carter hopped out of his cruiser, glad his shift was finally over. He had plans tonight with Mara. She didn't know that, but she would soon enough. He'd been planning this from virtually the moment he said goodnight to her Saturday evening. He wanted to make up for the way things ended. Even though none of it was his fault.

Carter opened the rear door and let Maverick out. The dog trotted to the interior door, ready to get his dinner and rest. Grasping the doorknob, Carter let them inside. Maverick ran in, toenails clicking on the hard floor. At a more sedate pace, he followed. Setting his phone on the counter, he went to the dog's kennel to get his bowl. He'd feed Mav, then go change clothes and gather up the things he bought to make dinner for Mara.

Dumping two scoops of dry dog food into Maverick's bowl, he added some supplements and a couple spoonfuls of wet dog food and stirred it all together. Maverick barked, eager for Carter to put the bowl down.

"Hang on, bud. It's coming." Holding the spoon out, he let the dog lick it, then put the utensil in the sink. Maverick ran to his kennel and sat, waiting. Carter put the bowl in the corner and left him to go change.

Taking off his utility belt, he stowed his gun in the safe in his nightstand, then headed for his bathroom. He turned on the shower and stripped out of his clothes, stepping into the hot spray to wash off the yuck of the day.

Not wanting to linger, he was in and out in five minutes. After drying off, he wandered into his closet and pulled on a pair of jeans and a sweater. Digging in his dresser, his hand closed around a pair of socks at the same moment he heard his phone trill from the kitchen. Maverick barked.

He hurried from his bedroom and picked up the device a moment before it would have rolled to voicemail. Ben's name flashed on the screen, and Carter bit back a groan. He hoped whatever reason his boss was calling didn't involve him coming back into work.

Answering it, he put it to his ear. "Townsend."

"Hey, Carter. I know you're off now, but there's been a shooting at Cullen Tate's house."

Instantly on alert, Carter's muscles tightened. "What? Are he and Piper all right?"

"Not sure, exactly. I don't have all the details yet. Just that it was Gustavo Herrera, and that Cullen was shot. I need you and Mav at the scene to help search."

Disappointment flooded Carter's belly that he wouldn't get to see Mara tonight, but he knew he couldn't say no to something like this. Nor would he want to. "Yeah. Give me a few minutes. I just changed out of my uniform. Can you text me the address?"

"Yep. I'll see you there."

The phone clicked as Ben hung up. Clenching his teeth, Carter blew a harsh breath through his nose, then glanced at Maverick, who sat at his feet, ears forward. "Ready to go back to work, boy?"

The dog barked once. Carter's mouth tipped up, and he shook his head. At least one of them was eager to go traipsing through the cold night.

He glanced at his phone, debating giving Mara a call. It would be nice to hear her voice. She didn't know he'd planned to come over, though. If he called, it'd just to be to deliver bad news. If he didn't call, she'd never know.

Growling, he shoved his phone into his pocket and spun on his heel to go change. No use upsetting her.

NINE

Maverick barked as Carter put his cruiser in park and got out. Opening the rear door, he hooked a leash to the dog's collar and led him into the equestrian center. He had an update for Mara about her car. It would have been quicker and simpler to call, but he wanted to see her. Especially after his plans to surprise her were dashed last night. They'd only texted a few times since she left his house Saturday evening, and it was now Thursday.

He was surprised at how much he'd missed her this week. Relationships weren't his thing. He wasn't a monk, but women were few and far between for him. They asked too many questions—wanted too many details about his past. Ones he didn't want to give.

But with Mara, it didn't matter how much he told himself she would eventually ask those questions; he couldn't keep her out of his mind. Even as busy as he'd been, she was never far from his thoughts. When things got slow, he found himself wondering if she was having a good day. Those were the times he usually sent her a text asking her how her day was.

And it didn't matter that his self-preservation instincts

told him to keep his distance. That she would make him open up about things best left buried. He simply couldn't stay away. She pulled him to her. Beckoned him with her fiery red hair, crystalline blue eyes, and pretty smile.

He wasn't going to lie, though. He was kind of glad work intervened with his plans yesterday. Sure, it would have been great to see her and spend time with her. But once he had a chance to think about it, his nerves crept in. She had him all tangled up inside, and he wasn't ready to unravel it all just yet. The part of him that wanted to keep his past under lock and key did a little happy dance at the change of plans, even if his body—and to be honest, his heart—did not.

Now, though, he was too tired to resist her pull. He and Maverick spent hours searching for evidence around Dr. Tate's house late into the night. Carter managed about three hours of sleep before he had to get up for his regular shift. Exhausted didn't begin to cover how he felt. His eyes never lost their grittiness today. Even Maverick felt the grind of the last twenty-four hours. There'd been much less barking in the car today as the dog snoozed between calls. Carter wished he could do the same.

Stepping inside, he pasted a smile on his face for the woman manning the check-in desk, Pam White.

"Well, Deputy Townsend. What brings you in?"

"I came to see Mara. Is she free?"

Pam smiled, a twinkle in her eyes. "Let me find out." She lifted the phone and punched some buttons, holding her smile as she asked Mara if she had time for a visitor. Hanging up, she pointed to the hallway to her right. "She's free for a few more minutes. You can go on back."

"Thanks." With a quick smile, he headed down the hall to Mara's office and rapped his knuckles on the open door.

She glanced up and smiled. "Hey. What are you doing here?"

Maverick whined, and Carter released him. The dog ran to her side, thrusting his snout under her hand.

She giggled, scratching his ears. Her melodic laugh sent a shot of desire through Carter's body, and he wished she were running her hands through his hair instead. Preferably while he kissed her senseless. He'd wanted to Saturday before the incident with her car. After that, the timing was never right. Not even when he took her home after the wrecker came and towed her car to the body shop. The mood was gone.

He sank into the chair across from her desk. "I have an update on your car."

Her hands stilled in Maverick's fur. "Oh?"

"The rock came from my neighbor's landscaping, but there were no prints on it. Another neighbor has a doorbell camera that caught a shadowy figure at the very edge of its field of view. But that's it. No car."

"So, was it someone from the neighborhood? A local kid?"

He shrugged. "Maybe. They could have had a car further down the road too."

"But why would they target my car and no one else's?"

That was the part that bothered Carter. "I'm not sure. Maybe they intended to break into several cars, but because yours had that glass break sensor, it foiled their plan and you were the only one hit."

Her brows dipped again for a moment before her expression smoothed out, and she nodded. "That makes sense."

"Yeah." Carter nibbled the corner of his mouth and glanced away.

"You don't think so?"

He turned his gaze back to her and blew out a breath, letting his misgivings go for now. "I don't know what to think. There's not much to go on, and we may never know who did it." He almost hoped that was the case. It meant it was random. He had no reason to believe it wasn't, but something about it bothered him. He just wished he could put his finger on what.

"So, how's your week been?" Mara spoke to him, but she looked at Maverick. "Did you catch any bad guys?"

The dog let out a short bark.

Mara smiled and ran a hand over his head again. "That many, huh?"

Carter chuckled. "We had a few busts. Nothing huge. At least not on shift. Gustavo Herrera came after Piper and Cullen last night."

Her eyes went wide. "What? Are they okay?"

He nodded. "They will be. Piper's unharmed, but Cullen took a bullet to the side. Just a graze, but it was enough to knock him down. I guess he hit his head when he fell, so he has a concussion too. Thankfully, it's nothing time won't heal."

"Wow. Is Herrera in custody, or did he get away again?" They'd all been following what was going on with Piper, Cullen, and the drug cartel. Mara was no exception.

"He's in custody. Cullen managed to knock him out, despite his injuries."

"Good for him."

"Yeah. The doc's pretty tough. So is Piper." He let out a sigh. "Other than that, it's been blessedly quiet. Just busy."

One corner of her mouth kicked up. "Isn't that word—quiet—anathema? Like it is for medical personnel?"

He shrugged. "I've never been one to put much stock in superstitions." Some of his military buddies swore by them—and lost their lives anyway.

"Me, either." She glanced at her watch. "I have a session to get to." She stood. "You're welcome to come back and talk with me a bit longer while I get set up."

Carter rose and called Maverick to heel. "Sure. I've only ever been beyond the offices once. That was for the auction."

Mara smiled. "Great. I'll give you a quick tour." She

rounded the desk and led him down the hall, then through the door leading to the arena and stables.

"I didn't know you conducted your own sessions," Carter said, his eyes trained on the therapists and riders walking around the arena. "I thought you were more of a paper-pusher."

She chuckled. "I don't, normally. I do a few here and there, but mostly I hide behind my desk nowadays. But I took on most of Gemma's patients while she's out. Thankfully, January and February are slow for me. All our end of the year stuff is wrapped up, and I don't have quarterly reviews until March." She rounded the corner into the stables.

Maverick's ears twitched at the sound of the animals. When he stuck his nose in the air and went on alert, Carter glanced around. Something had piqued his interest. "What do you smell, Mav?"

The dog's ear twitched his way, then faced forward again.

"It's probably just the horses."

Carter shook his head. "No. This is alert behavior." He unfurled the leash. "Mav, *such*."

"Zook? What does that mean?"

"Find." He kept his eyes on his dog as they moved a few feet down the corridor.

"What is he looking for?" Mara kept pace with him.

"Most likely narcotics."

"What? We don't use anything like that on the horses. Not even CBD rub. Why would he smell narcotics?"

Maverick stopped outside a stall before Carter could answer. The young man inside looked up, and the dog's butt hit the floor.

"Sir, I need you to come out of the stall, please." Carter motioned the man forward, who looked at him with wide eyes.

"Can I finish dressing Maisie down first? I'm almost

done." With the brush in his hand, the man motioned to the chestnut-colored horse.

"I'm afraid not. My dog alerted to the odor of narcotics. I need you to come out now."

The man's eyes darted between Carter, the dog, and Mara, who stood to Carter's right.

"It's all right, Scott. Just do as Deputy Townsend asks."

Carter could hear in Mara's voice that she thought this was some sort of misunderstanding. But from Scott's posture and the wary look in his eyes, Carter knew the kid knew he'd been caught. With what, though, remained to be seen.

Scott put the brush on the ledge and stepped forward, shoulders slumped.

"I'm only going to ask this once. Do you have anything on you? And before you say no, keep in mind, my dog knows you do."

The man's face fell. "Yeah." He reached for his front pocket.

Carter held up a hand. "I'll get it." He turned the man around. "Put your hands on the wall and spread your feet."

Mara made a strangled sound. Carter spared her a glance and saw her close her eyes and press a hand to her forehead. He felt bad about upsetting her, but was glad he was here to catch the guy. She didn't need drugs circulating here.

After a quick pat down, Carter recovered a bag of pills from Scott's pocket. He handcuffed the man and read him his rights, then turned him around and held up the bag. "What are these?"

Scott stared at them, lips pressed together.

"Oxycodone, right?"

Again, Scott said nothing.

"Where did you get them?"

"I want a lawyer."

Carter's shoulders sagged, and he lowered his arm. "Fine."

He stowed the bag in the pocket of his pants and grabbed Scott's arm. "Come on."

Mara stepped in front of them, her eyes glittering as she leveled a look at Scott. "Why? Why would you bring that stuff here? There are children here! You could have dropped one—or more—and one of them could have picked it up and ate it, thinking it was candy." She clenched and unclenched her fists, twin pops of color erupting on her cheeks.

Scott glanced away, his throat working. "I'm sorry, Ms. Mara. I didn't mean no harm. It was just a way to make some extra money."

Her eyes widened. "Wait. You're not just using it? You've been selling it?" She took a step forward, anger making her cheeks turn bright red. "You've been selling drugs out of my facility? To whom?"

The man clamped his lips together and looked away. Carter itched to ask him if this had anything to do with Herrera and the cartel hub they stumbled over a couple of weeks ago, but couldn't without the man's lawyer present. He'd make sure to look into that, though.

Mara made a disgusted sound in her throat as Scott continued to be tight-lipped, then moved out of Carter's way.

He paused as he walked past. "If you have sessions later, you might want to find someone to cover them. We need to bring in a team to search. Make sure there aren't more drugs hidden. You'll need to be available for that."

She nodded, crossing her arms, glare fixed on Scott. Fire shot from her eyes. "Fine."

Giving the man a soft push to get him going, Carter led him down the corridor, away from her.

"She was pretty mad." Scott's voice was soft.

Carter snorted. "You think? You're lucky she's a lady, or she might have clawed your eyes out."

"She was never supposed to know. Why did you have to show up and ruin everything?"

"This is not my fault." He pushed open the door leading to the main building and led Scott through. Maverick followed.

"Yes, it is. Everything was fine until you showed up." Anger in his voice, Scott tried to twist away.

Carter tightened his grip. "You don't want to run. Maverick's not just a narcotics dog." He made eye contact with the kid.

Scott blew a breath out of his nose, but complied.

"What in the world?" Pam glanced over as they walked past.

"Sorry for the disruption." Carter nodded at her and kept walking. He led his prisoner out the front doors and to his car. After loading Maverick into the backseat, and Scott into the front, he called for backup. Maybe there was something to that superstition about not saying the word quiet after all. What was supposed to be a pleasant lunch break just turned into a long afternoon.

TEN

Mara's phone chirped from the counter as she made dinner. With a quick glance, she saw her sister's name appear on the screen. Reaching over, she slid her finger over it to answer, then touched the speakerphone icon. "Hi. I'm making supper. What's up?"

"You want two kids? They come complete with their own attitudes."

A laugh bubbled out of Mara's throat. "Uh-oh. What did they do now?"

"I asked them to pick up their junk from the living room. You'd think I asked them to clean up the city dump. It took them an hour—an hour!—to put away their school stuff, two totes full of toys, and pick up the three cups and four bowls in my living room." Shauna finished with a huff.

Mara chuckled. "I'm sorry. Tell them I won't send them any Easter candy if they don't stop complaining."

Shauna scoffed. "Girl, they're past the stage of being bribed with candy. I've moved on to ice cream."

The doorbell pealed through Mara's house, and she glanced up from the skillet on the stove.

"Was that your doorbell?"

"Yeah." She looked toward the door, contemplating whether to just ignore it, not in the mood for visitors after the day she had. All she wanted was to make some comfort food and relax on her couch with some mindless fluff movie and forget that one of her employees had been trafficking drugs right under her nose. But when she heard a dog bark, her heart lifted as she realized who it was, and she turned back to the phone. "Hey, I need to go."

A short pause came over the line. "Wait. You said you're making dinner. Is it for two?" Shauna gasped. "Mara, do you have a date?"

Slowly, a smile spread over her face as an image of what awaited her on the other side of the door entered her mind. It wasn't an intentional date, but maybe an impromptu one. She hummed into the phone. "No comment."

"Oh, you better call me later. I need details about this guy. I didn't even know you were ready to date."

With a soft chuckle, Mara set her spatula down. "I promise to fill you in. At some point."

Her sister growled. "You better."

Mara giggled, then said goodbye. Pocketing the phone, she wandered down the short hall and answered the door. Carter stood on the other side in jeans, a t-shirt, and a fleece-lined corduroy coat. Maverick wagged his tail and barked again.

She smiled. "Come in."

They stepped inside, and Carter closed the door. "Hey." His smile ticked up one corner of his mouth, and his eyes held a watchful glint. "How're you doing?"

Mara sighed, understanding he wasn't asking just to be polite. He wanted to know how she was coping with what happened at the equestrian center. "Still annoyed. And angry that he duped me." She turned and led them into the kitchen, giving Maverick a quick scratch as she walked away. "Mostly,

I'm angry at myself for not noticing and putting all my employees and clients in danger. It's unacceptable." She went to the stove and picked up her spatula again, stabbing at the hamburger browning in the skillet. "Do you want to stay for dinner?"

"Sure. And don't beat yourself up too much, Mara. Drug dealers are good at concealing their activity." He took off his coat and draped it over the back of a chair at the table, revealing his navy blue long-sleeved tee beneath.

She stabbed the meat again. "I know. Doesn't change how I feel."

Carter took the spatula out of her hand and spun her around. She huffed and looked up into those liquid silver eyes that made her weak in the knees.

"The meat is dead, honey."

Her lips quirked. "I know that too. But it's safer to chop it into teeny tiny bits than it is to throw things."

A low rumble emanated from his chest. "Cheaper, too, I imagine."

"Very much so." She let her smile bloom, only to have it freeze on her face as their gazes locked and need built between them. It wouldn't bother her at all if he leaned in and kissed her right now.

He cleared his throat and glanced at the skillet, breaking the spell. "So, what are you making?" He handed her the spatula and took a step away.

Mara pursed her lips, disappointed, and turned to the stove. "Just spaghetti. I wanted something filling, but not complicated. Not tonight."

"Spaghetti sounds good. Can I do anything to help?" He shoved his shirtsleeves up his forearms.

She nodded toward a cupboard. "You can get plates out. This is done. I just need to mix everything together." Mara shut off the stove, then reached for the colander on the counter. She set it in the sink, then drained the noodles before dumping them back in the pan and adding the ground beef and spaghetti sauce. Using a noodle spoon, she dished out two plates and handed one to Carter. They each grabbed a glass of water, then went to the table in the corner of the kitchen and sat down. The dog laid down by the back door.

Mara twirled a forkful of spaghetti. "So, have you heard any more about who broke my car window?" she asked, choosing to focus on something slightly less irritating. Lifting her fork, she ate the bite. She'd been lucky and gotten her car back by the end of the next day.

Carter shook his head, twirling his own forkful. "No. Unless a witness comes forward, we're at a dead end. Have there been any other incidents?"

She shook her head.

"You haven't noticed anyone following you, or gotten any suspicious letters? No weird phone calls or hang-ups?"

"Nope." She cocked her head, chewing, and raised a finger. "Actually, I had a couple hang-up calls at the equestrian center this week, but I've gotten those there before."

"Does your phone log calls?"

She nodded. "I wouldn't be able to tell you which numbers they were from, though. I get calls from a lot of people whose numbers I don't recognize."

His brow creased in a frown, but he nodded. "If you get more, write the numbers down."

"You really think this wasn't random, don't you?"

Carter rested his fork on his plate, his mouth pulling down. "Yeah. I don't know why, but something's bugging me. Maybe it's all the trouble we've had here lately. The timing just feels—funny."

Her mouth flattened. She twirled another bite of pasta and brought it to her lips. Great. She wanted to chalk it up to some kid out causing trouble. More than likely, that's all it was, but his misgivings made her paranoid. Especially after he found her stable hand, Scott Sears, in possession of illicit drugs. She didn't know what to think.

But she couldn't do anything about it right now. And she was in the company of a handsome and interesting man. She didn't want to think about criminals and their stupid antics. "So, how long can you stay? Do you need to eat and run?"

He shook his head. "I can stay until you kick me out. My next shift isn't until Saturday."

Mara froze, glancing up at him from her plate. She knew he didn't mean that the way it sounded, but it didn't stop her mind from going to some naughty places. Ever since he almost kissed her last weekend, it had been at the back of her mind what it would feel like.

Carter gave her a chagrined smile and let out a soft chuckle. "That sounded—"

"Like a proposition?" She smiled.

He laughed again. "A little, yeah. I didn't mean it that way. Not that I haven't thought—" He broke off with a huff. "Never mind."

Mara giggled and raised another bite of spaghetti to her mouth. "I get what you're saying. And for the record, I've thought about it too." She slid the fork between her lips.

His eyes turned molten, and a fine shiver went through her. They were playing with fire. She needed to figure out quick if she was ready for what came next. Because going there with this man—she wouldn't be able to keep her heart out of it. And she wasn't sure she was ready to put it on the line again. A few dates and a burgeoning friendship were one thing, but falling for him? That was altogether something else.

They finished dinner and retreated to the living room, sinking onto the couch. Mara grabbed the remote and turned on the TV. "What do you want to watch? Or we could play cards?" She glanced over. Her heart flip-flopped in her chest at the heat blazing in his eyes, and her breath faltered.

He propped an arm on the back of the couch and reached out to toy with a lock of hair near her face. "I know we should pick some innocuous activity, seeing as this is our third date, but all I really want to do is kiss you."

Any air left in her lungs disappeared. Her body screamed yes, but her mind was locked on what it meant if she let that happen. She'd been able to pretend nothing was different. That her life wasn't about to shift into a new chapter. But if he kissed her—and she kissed him back—she couldn't hide her heart behind the protection of her widow status any longer. It would be out in the open—free to be damaged again.

But it would also be free to be loved again. She'd never thought she'd go through life alone. And the last three years had taught her alone was safe. But it was also lonely. She hadn't realized how lonely until Carter showed up. She didn't want to be lonely anymore.

Mara framed his face in her hands and leaned closer. She held his gaze, letting him see she was all-in. That there would be no going back. He lifted a hand to cup the back of her head and closed the gap.

Pillows. His lips were like pillows. It was the only thought that penetrated her brain as she savored the feel of his mouth pressed to hers. His touch short-circuited her ability to do more than experience the sensations now flooding her system. She shifted closer, wanting more.

His free hand landed at her waist, curling over her hip and up her back. Mara let her hands travel down over his shoulders and pressed them to his chest. Muscles flexed beneath her fingers. She moaned as his hand threaded through her hair.

Carter pulled back, breathing hard. "We should stop. This is moving a little fast."

She clutched his shoulders. "Is it?" It was, but that didn't mean she wanted to stop. Even though she knew they should.

He nodded. "I think we both need some time to think about where this is going—where we want it to go—before we take that leap."

Disappointment washed over her like a bucket of cold water, cooling the fire in her belly. He was right. Normally, she had better control of her body, but he short-circuited her thought processes, and her baser instincts took over.

She pushed against his chest, scooting back to put some space between them. "TV or cards?"

"Cards."

Mara said a prayer of thanks as she got up to retrieve the card deck that he chose the latter. Sitting there, attempting to concentrate on the television with him only feet away, would just lead to disaster. And a healthy dose of sexual frustration. At least cards would give her something to concentrate on besides how good he looked in that long-sleeved t-shirt and jeans.

ELEVEN

The digital clock on Carter's nightstand blinked as another minute ticked by. He rolled over and squeezed his eyes shut. It was too early—even for him—to get up. But the wind whipping through the eaves of his house woke him up about fifteen minutes ago, and he couldn't go back to sleep. Not because he couldn't tune out the sound, but because he couldn't tune out the thoughts running through his mind.

He almost hadn't left Mara's house. If she hadn't backed down when he said they were moving too fast, he wouldn't have argued further to stop her. It took every ounce of willpower he had to utter those words in the first place. She fired his blood and made him want things. Things he'd never dreamed of having. And it didn't matter what he did, he couldn't chase the thoughts away of what could be.

But that meant cracking open the vault around memories he'd buried all those years ago so he could stay sane.

He let out a snort and flopped onto his back. Who was he kidding? The vault was already cracked. What did that mean, though? He didn't talk about that time. Ever. The old adage was, "Time healed all wounds." Could enough time have passed to make the memories bearable now? Was that why his heart was driving him toward Mara? Was he ready to deal with the past?

Carter sighed and sat up, giving up on sleep. It didn't matter whether he was ready to deal with the past or not. He didn't particularly want to. And that was going to be his stumbling block with Mara. He knew there would come a day when he had to choose whether to protect himself from his memories and lose her, or break down his walls and let her in. Both prospects terrified him.

Getting out of bed, he rubbed his arms to ward off the early morning chill and walked to his dresser to get a pair of shorts and a t-shirt. He'd only planned on training with Maverick later, but since he was awake, he might as well do something productive and run a few miles on the treadmill.

Donning his clothes, he grabbed some socks and his shoes, then sat in the chair in the corner and put them on. Dressed for his impromptu workout, he left his bedroom to wander down the hall to the kitchen. Maverick lifted his head off his bed as Carter walked past the dog's kennel in the living room. He gave the dog the command signaling it was okay to leave his little cave, but Mav thumped his tail once and laid his head down.

Carter snorted, then chuckled. Smart dog. He knew it was too early to be awake.

In the kitchen, he threw together a quick pre-workout shake and downed it, then headed down the hall again to the spare room he used as a home gym. He took his earbuds off their charger and put them in, then tapped his watch to bring up his music app.

A sharp bark from the living room made him pause, his finger hovering over his wrist. He glanced at the door and removed an earbud. Maverick's low growl rolled down the hallway. Carter took the other earbud out and laid it on the shelf against the wall as he left the room. Senses on alert, he walked into the living room. His dog was standing near the door, staring at it as a menacing growl emanated from his chest.

Changing direction, he dashed to his bedroom and took his gun from the safe in the nightstand, then returned to Maverick's side. The dog hadn't moved.

"Maverick, *ruhig*." The growling stopped with the command to quiet. Gun at his side, Carter turned the lock on the door. He raised his weapon to the ready position and opened it.

Red paint stained his porch and door.

"What the hell?" He groaned. Their neighborhood troublemaker had struck again.

Not wanting to traipse through the evidence, Carter closed the door. "Maverick, *hier. Fuss*." He spun on his heel, the dog following in step as he made his way to the garage.

Carter flung open the interior door and smacked the button on the wall to raise the overhead door. At a steady clip, he advanced and ducked under it to hurry out to the street. Glancing both ways, nothing stirred. He paused, listening, but only silence greeted him.

Muttering a curse, he turned around and ran back to the house to call it in. He wanted to send Maverick out to track, but he needed better clothes and backup first.

After finding his phone and calling dispatch, Carter changed. He was pulling on his vest when Maverick's sharp bark told him his backup had arrived. Adjusting the vest straps, he jogged down the hall, calling Maverick to heel, and went out the garage door to greet his colleague. To his surprise, Ben walked up the drive.

"This was too weird for me to stay home. First Mara's car, now your door—" He shook his head. "I know it's probably just a kid causing mischief, but I've got a weird feeling."

"Same. Did you see if any other houses were hit when you drove in?"

Ben shook his head. "Everything looked normal."

The sinking feeling in Carter's stomach grew worse. Someone was targeting him. Sure, it could be a kid, trying to get his jollies by vandalizing the cop's house, but he couldn't remember seeing any teenagers in his immediate neighborhood. It was possible there was one a street or two over who knew where he lived. He jogged around the area with Maverick all the time when the weather permitted. But that meant the kid had to go out of his way to target Carter's house. This wasn't a spontaneous act. It was deliberate.

"I want to run with Maverick. See if he can pick up a trail."

"Sounds good. I'll stay here and maintain the scene until another unit gets here to take some pictures and samples."

Carter's head bobbed once before he turned and walked through the grass to his front porch, Maverick still glued to his side. He looked down at the dog, whose eyes were on Carter's face, ready for his next task. Carter didn't make him wait. He attached a long leash to the dog. "Maverick, *such*." He pointed at the ground in front of the steps.

Immediately, the dog turned away, nose to the ground by the stairs for several seconds before he took off through the yard. At the road, he turned left, on the scent of someone.

They ran about two blocks before the dog paused and stuck his nose in the air. Carter cursed. He'd lost the scent, which meant whoever vandalized his house probably got into a car here. He took note of where they were, then turned them around to go home. In a little while, he'd go knock on doors and ask if anyone heard or saw anything. Maybe he'd get lucky and someone would have a doorbell camera that caught something.

He ground his molars, hoping they found some clue to lead them to the perpetrator. Carter wanted to know why someone had it out for him.

TWELVE

Silence enveloped Mara as she pulled into Carter's driveway and shut the engine off. Gemma called her this morning and told her Ben rushed out of the house before dawn at the report of an incident at Carter's. She said he told her later that someone poured paint all over his front porch. Mara tried calling him when she had breaks in her schedule, but all she got was voicemail. He left one on hers, saying he'd try her this evening. She said screw that, stopped at Jester's for some barbecue to go and drove to his house. If he already had food, well, she'd eat, and he could put his in the fridge for tomorrow.

Opening her door, she snagged the handles of the food bag and her purse and got out. As she neared the front door, the dark stain on the porch floor and door—as well as the splatters on the surrounding brick—became visible. Her eyes widened as she took in the extent of the damage. It looked like someone dumped an entire paint can.

Mara reached out and rang the bell. It pealed inside, then a moment later the door opened.

"Mara." A smile erupted on Carter's face. "This is a surprise. Come in." He stepped back, and Mara entered.

Maverick stood from his spot on the rug by the fireplace and trotted over, nose working a mile a minute as he sniffed her and the bags she carried.

"You had your dinner." Carter shook a finger at the dog as he took the bag from her.

Mara giggled. "But ours smells better." She scratched Maverick's head.

"For sure." He turned and led her toward the kitchen. The dog retreated to his spot on the rug. "You didn't have to bring me dinner. I was just getting ready to heat up some stew."

"Well, now you can save it for tomorrow." She set her purse on the floor in the corner, then walked over to help him dish out the food. "So, what do you know about what happened out there?" She hooked a thumb toward the front of the house.

His mouth twisted. "Not much. Maverick tracked the scent a couple of blocks, then abruptly lost it. Whoever did it likely got into a car there. We canvassed the area for doorbell and security camera footage, but the only house with cameras is the one that caught the rock-throwing figure, and it's the other way down the street."

"Why would someone throw paint on your house?"

"Maybe because I'm a cop. Maybe because they're bored and played eeny, meeny, miny, moe." He shrugged. "I don't know. I do know, I'm installing my own security cameras. I ordered them this afternoon." A fierce scowl screwed up his face. "I don't know why I never put them in. As a cop and former Marine, I should know better."

"Well, it's not like Foggy Mountain is a hotbed of criminal activity." She frowned. "Usually, anyway."

"True, but crime can happen anywhere." He turned away,

getting plates from the cupboard. "But enough about all that. How was your day?"

Mara let him change the subject, not pushing for more details about his morning, sensing his frustration with the situation. "It was good. I stayed busy between sessions and paperwork. I put out an ad for a new stable hand too." She grabbed a serving spoon from the container on the counter by the stove and dished mac and cheese onto her plate.

"Yeah? That's good."

"Yep. The sooner I get someone hired, the happier we'll all be. I've been able to cover his shift through the weekend by offering overtime to my other hands, but his duties will fall to my therapists if I can't do that next week. And they have enough on their plates."

"Well, I hope you find someone quickly. I can come help out some if you need an extra set of hands." He took the mac and cheese she offered him, then nudged the pan of shredded pork toward her.

"I'll definitely keep that in mind. Though I'm hoping it doesn't come to me pleading for help from my friends." She tossed a grin at him as she forked meat onto her plate.

Once they had their food dished out, they retreated to the table and sat. Conversation stayed light, and Mara watched Carter relax as they ate and talked. She was glad to put some of the sparkle back in his eyes. They'd been rather cloudy when she arrived.

With their bellies full, they cleaned up their mess. When the last utensil went in the dishwasher, Carter closed the door, then turned to lean a hip against the counter.

"So, considering how things went the last time we sat in the living room after dinner, I'll leave it up to you what we do now. I have a few board games—somewhere. Or we can try watching a movie and see how that goes." Fire lit in his eyes.

Mara swallowed, sorely tempted to pick the movie option. But she'd never been one to rush into anything, and she was enjoying this getting to know each other period of their relationship. She didn't want to push things to a level they weren't ready for yet. No matter how much her body—and his, from the look in his eyes—wanted that. "What kind of games do you have?"

Understanding banked the fire burning in his gaze. "Monopoly, Pictionary, probably a trivia game. I'm not a hundred percent certain. I haven't played any of them since I moved here. And before that, game nights were few and far between."

"Same. Any of them sound good, though."

Maverick walked up and sat next to Carter, nudging his hand with his snout.

Carter glanced at Mara. "He needs to go out. I think all the games are piled in the spare bedroom closet—where my gym equipment is—if you want to go look."

"Sure."

They parted ways, and Mara wandered down the hall to the room he indicated, crossing to the small closet. She slid open the bifold door and glanced at the shelves. There were several boxes stacked across the top. Some of them were games, but others were just regular boxes.

A game she'd played before with Gemma and a couple of their other girlfriends caught her eye. It was fun. She remembered laughing a lot. Standing on her toes, she wrapped her fingers around its edges, working it free from the stack. She wasn't careful enough, though, and it knocked another box off. A small squeak escaped her as it bounced off the top of her head, then fell to the floor, breaking open and spilling its contents.

"Crud." Sighing, she stooped, setting the game down so she could clean up the mess she made. Mara did her best not to look at the pictures as she scooped them up. She didn't want to invade Carter's privacy.

"What are you doing?"

Mara squeaked again and glanced up. Carter stood in the doorway, that scowl from earlier back on his handsome face. "Sorry. I knocked this box off getting that game." She pointed to the game she picked. "I was just putting everything back."

"Oh." He walked into the room and crouched beside her. His hands brushed hers away. "Let me do it. You can take the game out and set it up."

She frowned at the edge to his voice. "Carter, is everything okay?"

"It's fine. Go set up the game."

Frowning, she hesitated only a moment before she picked up the box and stood, unsure what upset him. He couldn't be angry that she made a mess, could he? She was cleaning it up. And it was just a bunch of photographs. She'd noticed a few military ribbons in the box too. His posture reminded her of how he looked on their Valentine's date when he mentioned his military service. Something about his time in the Marines wasn't something he wanted to remember.

She wasn't going to pry, though. He'd tell her if and when he felt the time was right. Instead, she turned on her heel and left the room.

Thirteen

Carter let out a soft growl when Mara disappeared around the corner. Why didn't he just help her pick things up and pretend like it wasn't a big deal that his entire time in the Marines was splayed all over the floor for her to see? He'd forgotten this box was in here, or he wouldn't have sent her to pick a game.

But now, she no doubt had questions. Ones he didn't want to answer. He couldn't let her think he was mad at her, though. She'd done nothing wrong.

Shoving the last of the memories back in the box, he put it on the shelf and closed the door. Feet feeling like bricks of lead, he went to find her and apologize.

He found her in the living room. She'd taken a throw pillow off the couch and sat on it on the floor in front of the coffee table. Game pieces littered the wood surface as she set up the board.

Carter walked between the table and the couch and sat down. "Mara."

She glanced up. "You don't need to say anything."

His brow wrinkled.

Her eyes went back to the game pieces. "I understand that some things are harder to talk about than others. It took me a year before I could say Blake's name without tearing up. So, I get it. You don't have to talk about whatever memories that box of pictures brought back."

Carter twisted his hands together between his knees and glanced away, a giant lump in his throat. But not from the memories. Her easy acceptance that something haunted him touched him more than anything had in a long time.

He cleared his throat. "I appreciate that. I don't—can't—talk about that part of my life much."

"Have you ever tried a counselor?"

"No. I didn't have any PTSD. It didn't seem worth the time to tie up a therapist who could be helping someone far worse off than me."

Mara let out a soft snort. "You totally have PTSD. Not in the same sense as the men and women I see at the equestrian center, but you do in a way. Whatever happened over there scarred you. Enough that you avoid situations and conversations that would force you to talk about it. I'm guessing someone—or several someones—died."

Carter knew surprise lit his eyes, but her insight stunned him.

Her gaze flicked to his. "Don't look so shocked. Grief recognizes grief. You remind me of myself. Before I learned to deal with Blake's loss."

Damn. His brows dipped, and he glanced away again. "How did you deal with it?" He turned weary eyes on her. "How did you get past the pain and heal?"

She held his gaze steadily. "I talked to someone. Moving here and away from the memories in Oklahoma helped, but I still cried myself to sleep every night for six months. I finally decided that was enough. That I couldn't keep going like that, so I found a local therapist who specialized in grief and made an appointment. It took some time, but I eventually got to a point where the memory of his face didn't make me want to burst into tears. And at times, it even made me smile. I'd forgotten all the good times we had together, focusing instead on the pain his death caused. The hole in my life. My therapist helped me get back to the good memories."

He looked away again. The knowing look in her eyes called him out. Told him he knew she wasn't saying anything he didn't already know. And she was right. He did know that talking to someone would help him work through the pain and the guilt. He was just too chicken to do it. So long as everything stayed bottled up and buried, it didn't hurt as much.

But it was like a cancer, slowly taking over parts of his life that shouldn't be touched by memories of his past.

Like his relationship with her. His thoughts from the morning echoed through his mind. If he didn't talk about this stuff, he was going to lose her.

It was that thought that galvanized him to take a deep breath and utter words he hadn't even thought in almost seven years. "I killed my squadmates."

Fourteen

Mara fought to keep her face expressionless. She knew her eyes were round, but hoped no other signs of shock were present. "I'm sorry. Could you explain that?"

Carter ran a hand over his face and stood, pacing to the front windows to look out at the street. Mara didn't move, afraid to even breathe, lest she intrude on whatever war he waged with himself and made him close himself off again. She wouldn't pry, but she'd be lying if she said she didn't want to know what happened to scar him so.

"I was at the end of a six-month tour." His voice rumbled, low, throughout the room. "And so very ready to go home. It had been nothing but days on end of bright sunshine and sand." He stopped and shook his head. "So much damn sand." He swallowed, then took a deep breath and continued. "I was a minesweeper. I'd go out alone with just my dog, Bob, and clear roads for traveling generals and dignitaries, supply convoys—anything important. I got dumped out on a stretch of desert where intelligence indicated enemy forces had planted some mines."

"They just left you there by yourself?"

Carter looked at her and nodded. "It was a common occurrence. What I did was dangerous. No one could help me do it. The dog searched, and I controlled the dog. Once I found the devices, I either disarmed them myself or marked them for another team to come in and detonate or disarm them. It depended on the size of the field and what was going on in the area." He glanced away, focusing out the window once more. "Bob and I were out searching one night, doing our typical grid search pattern. In this instance, I was supposed to flag them for the EOD team." He shook his head. "Somewhere along the way, I messed up the grid. We found several mines, and I flagged them all." He lifted a shoulder, still staring out the window. "But we missed one. When the EOD team came to disarm them, one of the guys stepped on a mine."

Mara gasped and covered her mouth.

"The worst part was, it was near their vehicles, and they hadn't dispersed, so it killed three of them."

"Are you sure you missed it? Maybe the people who planted them came back and planted more." She doubted he'd left cameras surveilling the site after he left. Anyone could have come along and buried more mines later.

His brows knit together. "That's what the base commander said. It had happened before. But the thing was, when I went out that night, I knew Bob wasn't feeling the best. I wasn't the only one the desert heat and our schedule was getting to. We'd been on a stretch of nightly excursions because some of the top Marine brass were coming in. And just because we were working at night didn't mean we could skip training during the day. In between, we tried to sleep, but it's nearly impossible on a forward operating base. There's so much activity during the day." His shoulder rose again. "Anyway, they cleared me of any wrongdoing. I left the service six months later when my enlistment was up."

"But you still blame yourself."

He nodded, eyes trained out the window again. "They showed me pictures of the area during the investigation. I couldn't remember if we searched there or not."

Mara let out an inelegant snort. "Of course you couldn't. It was dark when you searched. And I bet the pictures were taken in the daylight."

Carter's head turned, the furrow between his eyes dipping lower. Uncertainty clouded his eyes.

Her eyebrows rose. "You never thought of it that way?"

"No. I mean, I knew I'd have a hard time recognizing anything since I was out there in the dark, but I didn't take into account the lighting difference in the photographs. The fact is, though, Bob and I weren't thorough enough. If we were—" His voice cracked, and he looked away, swallowing hard. "If we were, those three men would still be alive."

Mara's heart cracked at the pain in his voice and etched onto his face. All these years later, and he still felt it as fresh as the day it happened. She walked over and circled her hands around his bicep and leaned in. "Carter, tell me something. And I want you to be honest. Don't let your feelings cloud your answer."

His liquid silver eyes met hers, and he nodded once.

"When you went out that night—even knowing you and Bob were tired—had you ever searched tired before?"

"Of course. It's the military. Tired is a perpetual state of being."

She blinked up at him, pausing a beat to make sure he understood what he just said, then nodded. "And even though you were tired, did you do your job any differently that night? Skip steps or change things up?"

His frown deepened. "No."

"So why would you think you screwed up?"

He shifted his stance, uncertainty in his eyes, but he said nothing.

"Just because people died doesn't mean it was your fault. Or your dog's fault. I'm betting he missed stuff other times that someone later found, but you didn't get upset over that. Because no one died in those instances. And again, there's no evidence he missed the mine."

Carter's jaw worked, and he looked away.

Mara gave his arm a quick squeeze, then pushed back, but didn't let go. "Look, I'm not asking you to completely upend what you've thought—what you've felt—these last few years. All I'm asking is that you consider other possibilities to explain what happened."

He kept his gaze outside, but nodded.

"Good." She patted his arm and stepped back. "That's the first step in healing."

Carter barked a short laugh and glanced at her. "Are you using your therapist skills on me?"

A smile quirked her mouth. "Maybe." She sobered. "I'm not trying to make light of what you went through. Please don't take it as that."

"I'm not." He pushed away from the window and closed the gap between them to weave his fingers into her hair on the side of her head. "You're something special, you know that? Not only do you not run for the hills when you hear the mess going on in my head, you make me doubt the guilt I've lived with for over six years." He raised his other hand, framing her face as he tipped his head forward to touch his forehead to hers. "My battered soul doesn't deserve you."

The low rumble of his voice washed over her, and his words brought tears to her eyes. "Oh, but I do. I think we're meant to heal each other's brokenness." She lifted her hands to his face, feeling the rough beard stubble beneath her fingertips. It grounded her when the new feelings floating through her wanted to fly her away. Mara remembered this feeling. She was falling in love. But it wasn't the same as it had been with Blake. That had been fresh and exciting. This was warm, like a banked fire just waiting to be poked and explode into something bright and beautiful.

They stood there in silence, taking in the moment passing between them, until Carter's thumb drifted over her bottom lip. The fire inside Mara stirred. Her lips parted on a soft sigh.

He lifted his head, his silvery gaze connecting with hers, a question burning in his eyes. Mara stood on her toes and answered it, pressing her mouth to his.

Flames erupted in her soul. Every stroke of his hands on her body, every touch of his lips on hers fanned them higher until she clung to him like ivy. When he cupped her hips and tilted his pelvis into hers, she let out a long moan.

Carter pulled back, his silver eyes a deep greenish-gray. "I want to take you to bed and worship every inch of you. But if you aren't ready for that, we'll stop now."

Mara thought the first time she found herself in this situation would be awkward, and that she'd be nervous. She wasn't, though. And it wasn't. She was ready. Ready for *this* man. It had everything to do with him.

She threaded her hands into his sun-bleached hair and brought her face close to his. "I'm ready. I want you. All of you."

He attacked her mouth, taking it, and making it clear she belonged to him now. Mara had never felt possessed before by a man, but she did now. He'd taken full control, and she was just along for the ride. She couldn't wait to see where he took them.

Gathering her into his arms, he lifted her feet off the floor and walked through the living room and down the short hall, never breaking the kiss. Mara clutched his shoulders, loving the feel of his muscles shifting as he carried her. Carter's physique was impressive, and she couldn't wait to get her hands on it sans clothing.

They entered his bedroom, and he kicked the door closed on his way to the bed. He set her on her feet next to it and broke the kiss, then reached over to turn on the bedside lamp. A soft glow filled the room. Mara stared up at him, loving the way his eyes glittered in the low light.

"Still sure about this?"

She shivered as his voice washed over her. "Absolutely." Standing on her toes, she fused their mouths together again, toppling them onto the bed as she hooked her arms around his neck and pulled.

His soft chuckle rumbled through his chest into hers. She smiled against his lips, then moaned as his hands tunneled beneath her shirt and seared her bare flesh. In moments, her shirt and bra were gone, having disappeared over the side of the bed. She didn't mind. Not when he wrapped those large palms around her breasts and kneaded her sensitive flesh.

What she did mind, though, was that he still hadn't shed an ounce of clothing. Mara tugged on the hem of his long-sleeved t-shirt. Carter sat back and whisked the garment over his head.

She didn't waste any time. Eager to feel him without the cotton barrier, she reached out and ran her hands over his sculpted chest. Warm, silky skin over steely—but supple—muscles met her fingers. He was like one of those marble sculptures come to life. Mara traced the swells and valleys, raising goosebumps in her wake. She was happy to see she wasn't the only one affected by the other's touch.

With a growl, Carter took her hands in his and raised them over her head, holding them there while he bent his head to suck the tip of one breast into his mouth. Mara's lips parted on a gasp. She tugged on her wrists, but he wouldn't let go.

"Carter." She tugged again.

He raised his head. "Nope. Your hands are torture devices. If you touch the wrong spot, this is over before it starts."

She giggled. "I'm sure I could make it start again."

A grin slashed his face. "I'm sure you could too." His expression turned wicked. "But I'm having fun right now and don't want to take a break." He dipped his head again and took her other breast into his mouth.

Mara moaned again. Moisture flooded her core. *Dear God in Heaven.* If he was that talented with his tongue, she could only imagine what he could do with other parts.

Carter worked her into a frenzy. Sweat pricked her skin and waves of pleasure rolled through her, building into a tsunami that rose ever higher. Just when she thought she'd break, he sat up.

She huffed, making him chuckle.

"Patience isn't your forte, is it?"

Mara tugged on her hands again. "No. I want to touch you." Turnabout was fair play, after all.

He hummed. "Soon." His free hand drifted down her abdomen to the fastening on her khakis.

A whimper escaped her as his fingers brushed the skin beneath as he worked the button free. The zipper rasped, loud in the quiet room, as he drew it down. Then his hand was under the fabric, burrowing deep to find her center. Her hips bucked when he slid his fingers along her seam, discovering just how ready she was for him. She knew he could take her in one hard thrust and glide right in.

He seemed to know that, because his low groan filled the room as he slid a finger into her channel. Suddenly, her hands were free, and he was tugging her pants and underwear down her legs. Mara helped him, kicking her feet to free herself. As soon as they disappeared the way of her shirt and bra, she sat up and attacked the button on his jeans. Carter pushed her hands away and hopped off the bed, shucking the rest of his clothes.

Mara bit her lip. Those Roman sculptures had nothing on the man before her. She doubted any of them would look like him fully erect. She scrambled onto her hands and knees, crawling to the edge of the bed as he leaned over to fetch a condom from his nightstand. Mara took full advantage of his distraction. She wrapped a hand around him, stroking his silky steel shaft.

He jerked and let out a moan. "Mara."

She squeezed, eliciting another moan. Wanting to taste him, she leaned forward and took him into her mouth.

His hands landed in her hair, clutching the strands almost to the point of pain. He let go, groaning, when she bobbed.

Suddenly, she found herself on her back. Her body bounced as the mattress gave beneath her. Then he was above her, his handsome face contorted as he held onto his control with a fine thread. The condom wrapper crinkled as he tore it open. He had himself sheathed before she could do more than think about doing it for him. Her body wept as he nudged her knees apart and positioned himself between them.

"No going back, Mara. Stop me now. Otherwise, you're mine. This"—he tipped his hips forward, the end of his shaft bumping her entrance—"belongs to me. I don't share."

Her belly clenched. A deep, visceral need filled her. She never thought she'd be the type to respond to such an alpha statement, but holy hell if that didn't make her want to shoot off like a rocket. She raised her knees, making him press a fraction deeper. She swallowed, finding some moisture so she could speak. "It's all yours. Make it—make me—yours."

His mouth landed on hers. He thrust his tongue between her lips at the same moment he thrust his hips forward, impaling her. She let out a squeak of pleasure that got lost in their kiss.

Carter pumped into her, the exquisite friction doing things to her body she'd never imagined possible. Bit by bit, she unraveled until she could feel every separate cell. When he broke their kiss and gently nipped the end of her breast, the shockwave was enough to slam them back together and launch her into space. She let out a shout and dug her nails into his back, trying not to fly apart as wave after wave of euphoria ripped through her. Through her haze, she heard his guttural moan and felt his muscles harden until he felt like marble. Together, they collapsed, sinking into the bed as they fought for air.

The enormity of what they'd done hit her. His words from before echoed through her mind. No going back. He was right. There was no going back. The book on her previous life was officially closed.

Melancholy flooded her heart, but a sense of excitement quickly replaced it. If she had any doubt she was ready to move on, that feeling erased it. No matter what the future held with Carter, she was ready to face it. A part of her would always miss Blake, but she wasn't trapped in her grief anymore. She'd healed and was ready to see where life took her.

Carter rolled, bringing her with him. He brushed a strand of hair away from her face, his brows quirking as he saw her smile. "What's that look?"

Mara raised a hand to touch his jaw. "Nothing. Just me realizing how right this feels."

His expression smoothed out, and an intensity entered his eyes. "I never expected you. I'm happy you didn't stay home instead of coming to the auction."

Her smile widened. "I'll have to remember to thank Brooke for hauling me out of my house against my will."

His lips tipped up, crinkling his eyes. "For sure." He dipped his head, hovering inches away from her mouth. "Later, though. Much, much later."

FIFTEEN

Maverick's deep bark pulled Mara from sleep. She groaned and tucked the covers tighter around her shoulders, only to have them yanked away when Carter sat up.

"What?" She rolled onto her back and blinked, sitting up to grab the sheet and hold it to her chest, feeling vulnerable as she took in the sharpness to his features.

"He doesn't bark. Not randomly. There's always a reason."

He got out of bed and grabbed his jeans from the floor. They hadn't bothered to get dressed again last night. Mara hadn't left the bedroom, and he'd only left long enough to let Maverick out. She had enjoyed the sight of him walking away from her without a stitch covering his beautiful backside.

Donning his pants, he glanced at her as he walked toward the door. "Stay put. I'll be right back." He was gone before she could reply.

Mara blew a lock of hair out of her face, then got up. She had her underwear and his shirt on when he entered the room, holding her phone.

"It looks like you missed a call."

"Is that why he was barking?" She took the device and swiped the screen.

"From what I can tell, yes. Nothing seemed amiss outside. Who called?"

She frowned as she stared at the number. It wasn't local, but instead an eight-hundred number. Why would a solicitor call her before dawn?

The phone buzzed in her hand, and a banner appeared indicating the caller left a voicemail. She touched the screen and raised the device to her ear to listen. Her blood ran cold as the male caller's voice informed her the alarm at the equestrian center had gone off and the police had been dispatched.

"What is it?" Carter grasped her elbow, brows knitting together as he watched her.

She hung up and spun away, searching for her pants. "The alarm went off at the equestrian center. I need to go."

"I'm coming with you."

Mara didn't argue as he hurriedly got dressed. She pulled on her pants and exchanged his shirt for her bra and top. Snagging a hair tie from the pocket of her khakis, she pulled her disheveled hair into a messy bun and left the bedroom.

Maverick whined from his kennel when he saw her. She wanted to let him out but didn't, knowing the dog wasn't simply a pet. Dealing with him was something she and Carter needed to discuss as they moved forward in their relationship. But not today.

She found her shoes and sat down to put them on as he emerged from the hall. He'd added a belt to his jeans and attached a holstered pistol and his badge. A plain, black long-sleeved t-shirt stretched over his chest. Disappearing into the kitchen, he came back a moment later with his boots and sat down next to her to put them on. His fingers flew as he laced them up and tied them.

"Get your coat and purse. We're taking my cruiser, because I'm bringing Mav."

Mara nodded and dashed to the kitchen to get her things. Swinging her arms into the sleeves of her coat, she heard Maverick's nails tapping against the floor as he and Carter walked in.

"Ready?" Carter took his jacket off the hook by the door and put it on.

"Yes." She opened the garage door and stepped inside.

Carter slapped a hand on the wall, raising the garage door. The interior light came on as the door rolled up. He led them to the SUV backed into the far bay. It beeped as he unlocked it. Mara rounded the hood and climbed into the passenger seat. She was glad she parked behind his truck and not the cruiser.

The dog whined and let out a sharp bark as Carter loaded him into the kennel behind the front seats. She could hear him turn a circle. The driver's door opened and Carter got in, starting the vehicle. As they pulled out of the garage, he got on the radio and asked for information on the alarm. Mara held her breath as they waited for the dispatcher to contact responding units.

"Unit five-zero-nine, be advised responding unit reports open rear door. They are awaiting backup to make entry."

Carter raised the radio mic. "Acknowledged. Unit five-zero-nine en route."

Mara's heart kicked into overdrive. It wasn't a false alarm. She prayed the horses were all right.

Hanging up the mic, Carter flipped a switch and the lights and sirens came on. Maverick barked again and paced. His whines and short barks filled the silence in the cruiser as they crossed town to the equestrian center.

When Carter turned the corner onto the center's street, he shut off the siren. Two other police vehicles—both from the city department—sat in the parking lot. He pulled up next to them, calling into dispatch that he was on-scene.

Mara's knee bounced, her hand on the door handle, waiting for him to tell her she could get out.

He held out a hand. "Give me your building keys."

"What?" She frowned.

"You're not going in yet. Not until we clear it. And I don't want to break down doors to gain access from the front."

With a fierce frown, she stared at him for a long moment before letting out a huff and digging into her purse for her keys. They clinked as she dropped them into his open palm.

"Don't leave the vehicle." He opened his door, not waiting for a response.

Mara huffed again, but settled into her seat to wait. At least he'd left it running so she wouldn't freeze.

Sixteen

Carter loped toward the building's front door, Maverick straining at the end of his leash, to greet the officer watching the door.

"What have we got?" He reined his dog in and told him to sit.

The officer gave his attire a quick once-over, a curious frown wrinkling his forehead. "Signs of forced entry on the rear door. We were about to enter when dispatch told us to hold for you. This is city jurisdiction. Why are you responding? And off-duty, from the looks of it?"

Carter tipped his head toward his cruiser. "My girlfriend runs the place. She was at my house when the alarm company called. And extra hands—and a dog—are always useful at a burglary call. Plus, I have keys." He held up Mara's keychain.

The officer stepped back and motioned him toward the door. "By all means. I was not looking forward to sweeping up glass."

With a grunt, Carter flipped through the keys until he found the one that fit the front door. Unlocking it, he pocketed the key ring. "Stay behind me."

Nodding, the officer grasped the handle, speaking softly into his radio that they were ready to breach. When an affirmative came from the officer around back, he pulled the door open.

"Mav, *lauf.*" The dog lunged for the opening at the go command. Carter fisted the leash, holding tight.

"Ferris County K-9! Show yourself or you will get bit!" Carter waded deeper into the building, head on a swivel as they searched. He repeated the direction several times as they searched offices and conference rooms, then again, when they entered the arena.

A flashlight bobbed through the dark from the stables a moment before the police officer who came through the rear identified himself.

"Anything?" the officer with Carter asked his colleague over the radio.

"Negative. It's clear."

Carter grimaced. He led Maverick to the stables, wanting to run him along the stalls just to make sure, but doubted they'd find anyone. The building felt quiet.

After a walk through the stables, Carter confirmed it was empty. He took Maverick back to the cruiser and let him into his kennel.

"Well?" Mara peered at him through the slats from the front.

He shook his head. "Nothing. We haven't done a thorough search for damage, but no one's hiding in there."

"Are the horses okay?"

"They seem to be." He stepped back and shut the door after giving Mav some water. Rounding the vehicle, he opened her door. "Come on. I want you to walk through and tell me if anything looks out of place." He offered her a hand.

She took it and slid out of the car. Carter threaded his fingers through hers and led her inside.

Flipping on lights as she walked through the building, she surveyed every room up front. He could see her consternation build as nothing appeared amiss. It hit him as strange, too, that there was no damage. Who broke into a building like this and didn't take something or break something?

When they reached the arena door, she pushed through and made a beeline for the stables. Mara opened every stall and checked the condition of every horse. All of them looked fine.

Passing the stalls, she entered the feed room, where they stored all the hay, grain, and supplements for the animals. As soon as she stepped inside, she came to a quick halt. Carter put his hands on her shoulders to keep from knocking her down as he almost plowed into her.

"What's wrong?"

"Don't you smell it?"

He sniffed. "It just smells like hay."

"Exactly. Too much like hay." She walked over to the bales piled against the wall and touched one. "They're wet."

Carter frowned. "So?"

"So, wet hay grows mold. And mold is toxic to the horses." She groaned and covered her face. "This is a nightmare. I hope it's not all wet."

He walked closer and touched the hay. It was definitely damp. "Someone broke in and soaked your hay? Why?"

She dropped her hands. "I have no idea. But if we hadn't caught this, it could have been very, very bad. I could have a boatload of sick animals." She turned away. "I better check the grain too. And the supplements."

Moving toward the large drums along another wall, she pulled the top off one and stuck her hand inside. It came out covered in grain. She looked at him with tears shimmering in her eyes. "It's soaked."

Carter went to another barrel and took the lid off. He

didn't have to put his hand in to see the light reflecting off the water inside. The grain was swimming in this one.

"What am I going to do? All their feed is ruined. I have ten horses who will demand breakfast in just a few hours. Forget that I don't have the money on hand to replace all this. Where would I find it on such short notice?" She swept an arm out to encompass the room.

"Call Gemma. If anyone can find feed, it's her. She knows everyone. Your insurance should cover the replacement cost."

"Yeah, eventually. But in the meantime? I'm going to have to put it all on the business credit card and hope it doesn't max it out before they pay me back." She sighed and pinched the bridge of her nose, closing her eyes.

He reached out and squeezed her shoulder. Her bottom lip quivered, but she sucked in a breath and looked at him, steely determination in her pretty blue eyes.

Carter smiled. There was the fire he knew she had. He ran his hand down her arm and took her hand. "Come on. Let's go call Gemma. Get you some fresh feed."

Spine straightening, she nodded and followed him from the room.

SEVENTEEN

Phone tucked between her shoulder and ear, Mara rolled her eyes as the number she just dialed went to voicemail. She wasn't really surprised. It was Saturday. But that didn't change the fact that she needed grain for her horses.

A knock sounded on her office door, and she glanced up.

Brooke poked her head in. "Can I come in?" she mouthed.

Mara nodded and pointed to the chair in front of her desk as she hung up the phone with a disgusted sigh. "Hey."

"Hey, yourself. Gemma called. What the heck?"

"I know." She groaned and sat back, scrubbing her hands over her face. Her eyes were gritty, and she felt grungy. She hadn't been home yet to shower and change. Carter had to go into work, so he left her here to deal with the aftermath, promising to either get her vehicle to her as soon as he could or to find her a ride. To top it all off, a headache pounded behind her temples.

She sighed. "This is unbelievable. The police were here within five minutes of the alarm going off. And it's not like the perpetrator knew we had an alarm, or that it triggered. It doesn't sound in the building because of the horses. The only way they'd know is if they saw the control panels. Granted, they're right by the doors, but without the noise when it's tripped, I would think most people would believe the alarm wasn't armed." She shook her head. "How does someone do so much damage and get out of the building in less than five minutes?"

Brooke's nose wrinkled. "I don't know, hon. At least it was only the feed. They could have gone after the animals."

"Yeah. That's what I keep telling myself. It could have been worse. I just don't get why someone would want to do this. I buy all my feed local, so it's not like it's some farmer who's butt-hurt that I turned him down in favor of some online feed store. I'm just glad we found a few bales buried deep that didn't get soaked. It was enough to feed them this morning. I need the grain, though."

"That's why I'm here. Daddy's got some he can spare. It'll be here in an hour."

"What?" Mara sat up, wide-eyed. "Are you serious?"

Brooke nodded, smiling.

Tears swam in Mara's vision. She hopped out of her chair and ran around to give her friend a hug. "Thank you, thank you, thank you."

Giggling, Brooke hugged her back, then leaned away to look at her. "You're most welcome."

Dashing at the wetness on her face, Mara let out a soft chuckle at her weepiness. "Sorry. It's been a long day already. I'm exhausted."

"Don't worry about it." She waved a hand. "I'm glad we can help. I do have a confession, though."

"What's that?" Mara sat down.

The smile on Brooke's face turned sly. "A little birdie told me Carter showed up here with you at five a.m."

Turning as fiery red as her hair, Mara couldn't hold back the smile. "Your birdie was right."

Brooke let out a squeal and sat forward. "Really?"

"Yep. We were asleep at his place when the alarm company called."

Clapping her hands softly, Brooke did a little dance in her seat. "I knew it! When I saw the look on your face when he walked out on stage, I knew it would be worth every dollar I spent."

"I will be forever in your debt, I can tell you that." Mara sobered. "He's amazing. The last couple weeks—I've learned a lot about the state of my heart. I didn't think I was entirely ready to accept that chapter of my life was over. That I *could* move on. I think I was just waiting for the right man to move on with."

Brooke squealed again, wrinkling her nose as she expressed her delight. "Well, I'm glad." She slapped a hand on the desk. "This means we need to double date. Oh! No. Triple date. I'll call Gemma. I'm sure her parents would be thrilled to babysit for a couple of hours. Are you guys free tonight?"

"Tonight?"

Brooke lifted her hands. "Why not? It's Saturday."

"Um, I'll have to check with Carter. He had to work today, so he might not want to go out tonight."

"Oh." Brooke's nose wrinkled. "Okay. Next weekend, then." She pointed a finger at Mara. "Let me know."

"I will." And she would. Going out as a group sounded fun. She missed being part of a couple and doing things with other couples. It was no fun being the third wheel all the time.

"Perfect." Brooke sat back and glanced around the room. "Girl, we need to redecorate. This place is dull."

Mara laughed. "It is not." She agreed it was plain, but it wasn't dull. Her artwork—painted by Gemma's sister-in-law

Laurel—brightened up the space and kept it from being boring.

"Yes, it is. Except the art. That's gorgeous. You need stuff to compliment it. As much time as you spend in here, you'd think you'd have put up more decorations by now."

"Honestly, I think about adding things sometimes while I'm sitting in here, but then I go home and my brain dumps everything." She shrugged. "I figure if I see something I want enough that would go well in here, I'll buy it."

Brooke narrowed her eyes and hummed.

Mara shook a finger at her. "Don't you dare buy me anything else. I don't need another present from you for the rest of my life. You've spent quite enough on me."

The other woman giggled. "I told you at the auction, I'll spend my money however I please."

Rolling her eyes, Mara sighed. "So spend it on more worthwhile causes."

"Your happiness is a worthwhile cause."

"Decorations won't make me happy."

"Maybe not the way you're thinking."

"Brooke."

With a wide grin, her friend waved her hands. "Fine. No decorations. Until your birthday. Then all bets are off."

Mara sighed again and decided it was time to change the subject. "So, can you give me a ride back to Carter's to get my car once the grain arrives? We came in his cruiser, since he brought Mav. It'll save him having to get it to me or finding me a ride back."

"Sure." A wicked smile appeared on her face. "We should have some retail therapy today. I think you need it."

Groaning, Mara slumped in her chair. One way or another, Brooke would get her to decorate her office today. And since she didn't really have anything else to do besides catch up on laundry and pray someone called her back about grain for next week, she was free until Carter got off work this evening. There was no use making up an excuse. Brooke would sniff out a lie in a second.

"Fine. But I'm driving. And after I take a shower."

"Deal."

Eighteen

Carter jogged up the walkway to Mara's house, Maverick at his side. They hadn't made plans, but he didn't care. He'd run home long enough to shower and change, then got in the car and drove over, eager to see her. She'd updated him a couple of times during the day on the situation at the equestrian center, but he needed to see her. To touch her.

Last night flipped his world on its axis. Not just the sex —that was incredible—but the emotional connection. He'd been telling the truth when he said he never expected her. Or that he didn't deserve her. Her easy acceptance of his demons—as well as her words about looking at it from a different perspective—lit up a path he'd never envisioned before. And he'd be damned if he didn't walk down it. He could see his future beckoning him from the other side. It was beautiful. More than he ever thought he'd have. He wasn't giving it up.

Ringing the bell, Carter waited for Mara to answer. This two-house thing was going to get old quick. Normally, he didn't want a woman in his space, but with Mara, it wasn't like that. He didn't want it to be just his space now. Moving in together at this stage was much too soon, but it wouldn't be long if they kept going the way they were.

The door swung open, and he smiled, drinking in her pretty face. "Hey."

Returning his smile, she stepped back. "Hey, yourself."

Carter ushered the dog in, then followed and shut the door. He snagged her around the waist and hauled her close. She let out a squawk of surprise and grabbed his arms. Her wide, bright blue eyes met his, then crinkled at the corners as she smiled.

He grinned, bending his neck to bring his lips within millimeters of hers. "Hi." The word was barely out before his mouth crashed down, and he swallowed her soft gasp. Fire erupted in his veins, surging south and short-circuiting his brain. Using the few remaining brain cells still firing, he pulled back before he pushed her against the wall and they had a repeat of last night. That wasn't why he was here. Well, not the only reason.

"Sorry. Didn't mean to ambush you as soon as I walked in. But I've been thinking about that most of the day."

She smoothed a hand over his jaw. "Don't apologize. I've been thinking about it too."

He leaned in and pressed another lingering kiss to her lips before stepping back. "So, did you eat?"

"Yeah. Brooke and I went into Asheville." She walked into the living room, stopping near the coffee table. "She decided I needed retail therapy and that my office needed a makeover." Mara gestured to the bags on the couch. "I haven't been back too long. We didn't leave the equestrian center until lunchtime. And there's no, 'Let's just pop into a couple stores quick,' with Brooke. The woman could be a professional shopper. Once we finished putting a dent in my wallet, we went to dinner."

"Did you have fun, at least?"

"Always. She's a blast to be around. Speaking of, she invited us on a triple date with her and her fiancé. Gemma and Ben are coming too."

"When?"

"Probably next weekend."

His head bobbed once. "Sounds good. I'm off Friday and Saturday."

"I'll let her know. Do you want something to eat?"

"I can go get something." He didn't come here to have her feed him, either.

She waved a hand. "I was going to make you a grilled cheese sandwich. There are chips in the pantry."

"That works."

"What about Maverick? I know he can't eat grilled cheese, but did you feed him before you came, or are you going to run out on me soon?" She glanced over her shoulder as she led him into the kitchen.

"He ate while I was in the shower."

Her eyes took on a heated look. "Does that mean I get you all night?" She stopped next to the island.

He kept walking until he was within touching distance. "Do you want me all night?"

The heat in her eyes grew, and she sucked her bottom lip between her teeth and nodded.

Carter's pants grew tight as he swelled behind his fly. "Then, yeah. You get me all night."

She held his gaze a moment longer, before quickly spinning away and marching over to the fridge. "Well, then, let's get you fed. You're going to need the energy."

He bit his tongue to stop himself from telling her to forget the food—that he'd eat later. But he didn't want their relationship to be all about sex.

Clearing his throat, he pulled out a seat at the island and sat down. "So, did you get your feed situation sorted out?"

Mara grimaced as she dumped the ingredients for his sandwich on the other side of the island. "Kind of. Brooke got her dad to donate enough to get us through the next few days. I put in calls to all the other places I order from. But it's the weekend, so no one has called me back yet. We're good until Tuesday. After that—well, I'm trying not to think about how many calls I'll have to make and the overnight shipping charges I'll have to pay if I can't source grain and hay locally by then. Although, hay isn't really the problem. I know I can get that once I can get someone to call me back. But I have a few horses that really need the grain or they drop weight quickly." She slathered butter on two slices of bread as she talked, then laid one in a skillet before adding cheese and the other slice of bread.

"Did you contact your insurance company?"

Mara turned, leaning her back against the counter and bracing her hands on either side of her hips. "Yeah. The claims process is rolling. Hopefully, it won't take too long. Did you hear any more about who may have done this?"

Carter blew out a breath. "No. All the facility cameras caught was a hooded figure picking the lock on the back door. The person was slight, so they think it might have been a woman."

"What? A woman? Seriously?"

He nodded. "Have you fired anyone lately? Or had a disgruntled patient? Or the parent of a patient?"

"The officer in charge of the scene asked me the same questions. No. I can't think of anyone who would have it out for either the center or for me, personally, except Scott Sears. But he's not slender enough or small enough to be mistaken for a woman." She pushed away from the counter and opened a drawer, taking out a spatula. Using it to lift the edge of the bread, she checked the bottom, then let it back down.

Carter watched her, mulling over the case. It struck him as

odd that three vandalism incidents in the same week were random. Especially when two of the three involved Mara. Even the paint incident could involve her, since it was in the same location as another one.

Like a hammer to the head, it hit him that the common denominator might not be Mara. It might be him. But he didn't have any better of an idea about who could be out to get him than she did. He was certain there were people out there he'd put away on the job who would love to do him harm, but no names were coming to mind. Not that fit the description of the person in the video, anyway. Tomorrow, he would go through his old cases and talk to Ben. Maybe they could figure out a suspect pool. Something needed to give before someone—namely Mara—got hurt. If this was about him, she was caught in the crossfire—a place he didn't want her to be.

"What's that look?"

"Huh?" Carter snapped out of his thoughts.

She held up the spatula and pointed it at his face, waving it in a small circle. "The look on your face—what is it? You looked like you were thinking hard about something."

"Oh. Yeah. It just hit me that this might be about me."

"You?" She frowned. "Why would they target my horses, then?"

"I don't know. But the first two incidents happened at my house. One of them you weren't even there for."

"Right, but you weren't at the equestrian center, either."

"No, but I visited there." He paused as he thought about his previous visit. "Did your stable hand make bail?" Even if he was too large to be the person on camera, it didn't mean he wasn't there, or that he hadn't convinced someone else to break in.

Mara's eyebrows dipped. "I don't know. It could be him, but he doesn't fit the description."

Another thought struck Carter. "And the first incident was before I busted him."

Her shoulders slumped. "Never mind. I guess he's not our guy."

"It's possible that one is unrelated. It could have just been a local kid, out causing mischief."

"Maybe." She lifted the corner of his sandwich again, then flipped it. Butter sizzled as the other side heated. "I just hope someone figures it out before more happens. I'm worried next time someone will get hurt."

He walked up behind her and curled his hands over her shoulders. "I'll do some digging tomorrow. See if I can't shake something loose. But tonight, I refuse to think about it anymore."

She turned her head, bringing her lips within inches of his. Carter couldn't resist the pull and kissed her. Somehow, he held onto his restraint, and gentled the kiss. Lifting his head, he sighed. "That sandwich almost done?"

Mara giggled and turned around. "It's close enough."

"Good." Because he was hungry, but for much more than just food.

NINETEEN

Maverick's toenails clicked on the hallway floor alongside Carter's footsteps as they walked toward Ben's office. Rounding the corner, Carter paused and rapped his knuckles on his boss's door.

"Come in." Ben's voice carried through the wood and glass.

Carter twisted the knob and stepped into the doorway.

"Hey." Ben looked up with a frown. "What are you doing here? You're on the evening shift tonight, aren't you?"

"Yeah. I wanted to talk to you, though. And do a little research."

"Oh?" Ben sat a little straighter. "Have a seat." He motioned to the chair in front of his desk.

Stepping deeper into the room, Carter sat down. Maverick laid down next to him.

"What's up?"

"So, I've been thinking about the vandalism. Both at my house and at the equestrian center. The city department has mostly been looking into Mara, since two of the three directly involved her. I want to look at me, though. Past cases I've worked, people I've put in jail who could hold a grudge. I think it would be smart to take a closer look at Scott Sears too."

"Hold up." Ben waved a hand. "This is the city's case. I can't just throw my hat into the ring and start investigating."

"I know. But that doesn't mean I can't do a little of their legwork and give them some suspects."

"You can give them your opinion, but they're still going to go through all your old cases in case there's someone you didn't think of who actually has a solid motive and means."

"Right, but at least this is a place to start."

Ben sighed and sat back, folding his hands over his chest as he stared at Carter. "You really think this is about you?"

Running a hand over his jaw, Carter glanced out the window, then at Ben. "I know I don't have anything to support it, but yes. The paint was on my house, not Mara's. If this was about her, wouldn't it have been her house?"

"True, but there's also nothing to say the incidents at your house are connected to the equestrian center. You brought up a valid point in Scott Sears. I've been keeping tabs on him—my wife does work for the place where he was trafficking drugs —and he made bail the day after his arrest."

Carter's eyebrows drew together. "Who posted it?" With the charges the kid was facing, it had to be several thousand dollars.

"He did."

"Bullshit." There was no way a stable hand had that kind of cash.

"That's what I said. But the money came from his bank account. And I don't have a reason to subpoena his bank records to find out where he got it. Yet. That might come from the feds, though. I called Agent Porter—the ATF agent leading the task force formed after the bomb in Piper Riordan's car—and alerted him to Sears. He called his DEA counterpart, and they posted an agent on the kid, hoping to catch him meeting with other cartel members."

Carter let out a snort. Maverick lifted his head and tilted it, then laid back down with a sigh. "Would he really be stupid enough to meet with them now?"

Ben shrugged. "He was dumb enough to bring drugs to work, knowing the sheriff's wife worked there. Who knows? Tristan and Jake are working things from our end, and Porter promised to share anything the task force discovers."

"Good. So, that just leaves the incidents at my place."

"I know I can't dissuade you from digging into your past cases. Just make sure you turn over *all* your cases to the local police and not just the ones you like for this."

"Will do. I plan to check with Fort Carrington too. See if anyone I put away there has it out for me. There were a few who I can see holding a grudge long enough to come after me after they served their time."

Ben's head bobbed once, and he sat up. "Sounds good. Thanks for the heads-up."

Carter stood. Maverick got to his feet and shook, ridding himself of sleep. "Yep." His mind was already on who he would look up first as he turned and headed for the door.

"Carter."

Pausing in the doorway, he glanced back. A pit formed in his stomach as he took in the fierce frown on Ben's face.

"Watch your back. And Mara's. This is connected to one of you, and the frequency of the acts bothers me. Whoever's behind this will strike again, and they're going to get bolder each time."

That pit turned into a gaping hole. "I know. That's what I'm worried about too."

Ben's mouth flattened.

"I ordered a security system for my house. Cameras and window and door alarms. And I paid for expedited shipping. Do you think you can come help me put it up when it arrives? It's supposed to come in on Tuesday."

"Sure. I'll grab Tristan and Jake too. The four of us should be able to get it set up pretty quickly." He let out a soft snort and shook his head. "Who'd have thought it would be the K-9 unit who has trouble with a vandal?"

Which was exactly what had Carter worried. Most run-of-the-mill vandals wouldn't come near him. Maverick's loud, deep bark would send them running. Whoever this was either had it out for him, or they liked the adrenaline rush that came with targeting a K-9 deputy. Both scenarios meant there would be more incidents, and he wanted to be ready.

"Well, hopefully, we can catch them in the act next time." He took a step back. "I'm going to see if I can come up with some suspects. I'll let you know if anything turns up." At his boss's sharp nod, he spun on his heel and headed for his desk, Maverick at his side. He had some digging to do.

The casters on his chair clacked as he rolled it back and sat down. With a low groan, Maverick climbed into the dog bed next to the desk. Carter's mouth quirked as he glanced at the dog. He would owe the animal a run later so he could burn off the energy he was storing up now.

Turning, he picked up the phone and made a call to his old boss. After explaining the situation, the man promised to have an officer compile a list and forward it. Carter was grateful for email. That list was likely to be a long one.

With one department taken care of, he turned his focus to his current location and logged into the department's system to run a search of his cases. Right away, several jumped out at him. There were some perpetrators he'd never forget. Jotting their names down on a steno pad, Carter started sifting through the less memorable cases and came up with a few possibilities. He ran all the names to get their current status and found several who were out of jail. They went into a separate column.

Sitting back, he stared at the pad, twirling his pen through his fingers. Details from each case swirled through his head as he read the names. One of them made him pause as he remembered something. Dustin Spalding had run from him on foot at a traffic stop because he had a felony amount of marijuana in his car. Carter had chased him down, using Maverick to bring him to a halt when he refused to stop. It wasn't Dustin, though, that he remembered well. It was the man's wife, Amy. That woman was crazy. She'd vowed revenge, arguing that her husband shouldn't have his life—and subsequently hers— ruined for a little weed. It didn't matter to her that he broke the law. She saw Carter as the bad guy.

He wrote her name on the list. Going through it once more, he focused on known family members, but Amy Spalding was the only one who stuck out to him. Her wild behavior fit with the pattern of vandalism at his house. The equestrian center was the outlier. It felt more planned and less like the impulsive act of someone angry at the police.

Sighing, he rubbed his forehead. It was definitely possible they were unrelated. Scott Sears had a strong motive for vandalizing the equestrian center. Either way, they had some viable suspects for all three incidents.

Carter opened his email and typed his list into a message to the detective in charge of the vandalism at his house. At the last moment, he copied Tristan and Jake. It was unlikely any of the people he listed would be responsible for the ruined horse feed, but he wanted to cover all his bases.

Having done as much as he could for now, he pushed away from his desk. Maverick lifted his head.

"Let's go for a run, Mav." The dog needed the exercise, and Carter needed to clear his head and get rid of the antsy feeling plaguing him. This wasn't over, and it was driving him insane that he couldn't do more to catch the person wreaking havoc on his and Mara's lives.

TWENTY

Car doors slammed, drawing Carter's attention away from the sensor he was attaching to his bedroom window. Climbing off the ladder, he left the room and headed for the front door to let his helpers inside. He threw open the door as Ben, Tristan, and Jake walked up the path. Tristan carried a ladder while Jake held a drill, and Ben had a toolbox.

"Hey, guys. Thanks for coming." He stepped back to let them enter, then closed the door.

"Not a problem." Ben smiled. "Show us your setup."

Carter led the men to the kitchen, where he'd laid the system out on his dining table. "Some of the sensors I've already installed." He'd started as soon as it arrived this morning, knowing he could do those on his own. "I was just finishing my bedroom window when you guys arrived. I still need to do the garage windows, but all the others are done. And the doors. I haven't done those yet, except that one." He pointed to the back door. "I haven't touched the cameras. I need help with the angle on those and with running wires through the attic."

"You know, they have people who install these things for a living," Tristan quipped.

Carter shrugged. "I didn't want to wait two weeks."

"Fair enough. Let's get busy."

Grinning, Carter laid out where he wanted the cameras. They decided to split into two teams to make things go faster. Tristan and Jake took the front of the house, while Ben and Carter tackled the back. They were going to mount everything, get it hooked up, then check the angles on the app that came with the system.

The back of Carter's house was one long straight line, so he opted for just three cameras for the back. One motion-sensitive camera that would rotate on each corner and then a third, smaller, fixed camera over the back door. The front would be trickier because of the porch, but once they were done, every inch of the home's perimeter would be covered.

Ben set the ladder up on the far corner of the house. Holding his drill, Carter climbed up with the template that came with the kit and drilled holes to mount the camera bracket.

For the next two hours, they worked to install the cameras. It was a much more involved process than Carter thought it would be, and he was glad Ben brought Tristan and Jake to help. They'd have been setting up floodlights in the yard so they could see to finish if it weren't for the extra hands.

Once all the cameras were up, Carter went up into the attic and attached the wires to the floor joists with a staple gun, running them all to the area over his closet. He'd already scouted the spot where he wanted to put the central data hub. His closet had an outlet in it, so he'd cut a hole in the wall beside it. The plan was to run the cables down through the wall and attach them to the hub in his closet.

One by one, he sent the cables down the wall to Ben, who used a bendable flashlight and a pair of long needle-nose pliers to pull the cables through the hole. When all the cables were down, Carter left the attic and headed to his room.

"How's it looking?"

Ben glanced up from where he crouched in the closet. "Good. We get the last of the window sensors installed and I'll turn it on."

"They're done." Jake entered the room and peered around Carter at Ben. Tristan came up behind them.

Carter walked to his dresser and picked up his laptop. The system had a router and would run without the computer, but they needed it to set it up. Opening the lid, he crouched next to Ben. They plugged the hub in to both the wall and the computer, and Carter pressed the power button. Lights flashed as the system booted up, and the screen on his laptop changed as the software opened.

"Damn. I need this in my house," Jake said.

"You do." Tristan glanced at his partner. "We've got something similar, and it's nice."

"Same here," Ben said. "Except I didn't have to install mine." His lips twitched, and he poked his tongue into his cheek as he glanced at Carter.

"Time crunch, remember?" Carter raised an eyebrow, fighting his own smile.

Chuckling, Ben turned back to the computer.

It didn't take them long to verify everything was working. They were into the easy part. The software did all the heavy lifting.

Carter clicked on the menu, then the link for the camera feeds. They looked pretty good. He was glad he went with the fisheye style. They rotated faster and had a wider field of vision. As they watched, the camera on the left rear corner of the house turned. It had picked up on Maverick running around the yard.

"I'd say it's working." Ben glanced up.

"Yep. Awesome." Carter let out a breath, some of the weight he'd carried for the last week and a half lifting. The system might not stop someone from vandalizing his property again, but it would help him catch them. He finally felt like he had a leg up in this case. Closing the lid, he glanced at his friends. "Thanks, guys. I appreciate the help."

Ben slapped him on the back. "You're welcome. Now, what are we doing for dinner? I'm starving."

Chuckling, Carter led them out of the room. "How about Jester's? My treat."

Twenty-One

Mara swiped her hands on her skirt just before she reached for the doorknob to let Carter in. She didn't know why she was so nervous. It wasn't like this was their first date. But it was a test of their relationship. They were socializing as a couple. The only thing more momentous than that at this stage would be revealing him to her family. She still hadn't done that, despite Shauna's best efforts to get information out of her. Every time she tried, Mara managed to change the subject. She knew she needed to clue her in, but she didn't want the phone calls and questions sure to come from her brothers. Not yet.

Grasping the knob, she twisted it and opened the door. Her nerves dissipated as she drank in the sight of the man on the other side. In dark slacks and a light-gray button-up under a black leather coat, he looked good enough to eat—and she planned to lick him later. She'd do it now if she thought they had enough time. But they were supposed to meet the others in less than an hour at a restaurant in Asheville.

He smiled and walked inside, sending shards of white-hot

need to every nerve-ending in Mara's body. They might be a little late to dinner.

"Hey, babe." Carter leaned down to press a quick kiss to her lips.

Mara clutched his shoulders, then forced herself to let go. As much as she wanted to strip him naked, she really didn't want to explain to Gemma and Brooke why they were late. Both women would be merciless in their teasing. So, instead, she stepped out of his arms and opened the closet door to get her coat.

"Don't cover up on my account." Carter's voice held a slight rasp.

Mara glanced back to see the banked fire in his eyes as his gaze traveled over her.

She shivered, but it had nothing to do with the chill she'd let in with him. "Don't look at me like that. I'm trying hard not to say screw it to dinner and drag you down the hall to the bedroom."

The fire flared to life, turning his eyes to molten silver. "I'm okay with that."

Mara smiled and zipped her coat. "I figured. But I'm not calling Gemma to tell her we aren't coming because I need to ride you like my horse."

His jaw worked and the blaze in his eyes grew hotter. He stalked toward her until he was only inches away. "And how do you ride your horse?"

She licked her lips, subconsciously anticipating the taste of him. "Fast and hard."

Carter's hands shot out to grip her waist. He backed her toward the wall. "We've got time for fast and hard." His mouth crashed onto hers.

Mara's resolve fled, and she thrust her hands into his hair. He found the zipper on her jacket and pulled it down. She flapped her arms, freeing herself. As soon as the coat hit the ground, he lifted her, pressing her to the wall, his hands under her thighs. Mara groaned and wrapped her legs around his waist.

His mouth left hers to travel down her neck. "I like that you wore a skirt. Easy access." His fingers drifted around her leg to run along the edge of her panties. He dipped a finger beneath, making her groan again.

She ground against his hand. "Don't tease me. Fast and hard, remember?"

"Yes, ma'am." He removed his hand. Gripping her hips, he turned, heading for the living room.

"Where are we going?" She figured he would just take her against the wall. They'd done that several times already.

"You said you wanted to ride me like your horse." He stopped in front of the couch and lowered her feet to the floor. Stepping out of her arms, he reached for his belt.

Mara heard the clink of his belt buckle, then the soft rasp of his zipper coming down. Heat made her body flush as she watched him lower the zipper, then remove his pants with one swift tug.

A wicked smile lifted up one corner of his mouth. "Your turn." He reached beneath her skirt and hooked his fingers in her panties, pulling them down her legs.

She stepped out of them, then put a hand in the center of his chest and pushed. He plopped onto the couch, and she followed him down, straddling his waist.

His hands grasped her hips, holding her over him. The tip of his shaft teased her entrance. "You ready?"

She offered him a jerky nod, wiggling her hips. "Yes," she said, voice breathy.

The word was barely out of her mouth when he thrust up, impaling her. Mara let out a sharp shout of pleasure at the invasion, but only took a moment to recover before she did exactly what she said she wanted to and rode him like her horse. Hips moving in time to his thrusts, he brought her to the brink. When she neared the top, he lifted the hem of her sweater, pushing it and her bra out of the way to latch onto her nipple. It was enough to send her soaring. With a loud cry, her orgasm crashed over her, spreading goosebumps along her body in waves. Pleasure pricked her scalp and made her ears ring. Vaguely, she heard his harsh grunt and felt a soft bite on her breast as Carter's climax hit.

Boneless, she collapsed against his chest, struggling to catch her breath.

"I think I'm jealous of your horse. He gets to have you ride him every day."

Mara giggled and lifted her head. "You're much more fun to ride."

"Good." His hands, which still held her hips, rose to stroke her back.

A thought hit her, and in her pleasure-soaked brain, she didn't stop to think about it. "We should talk about how we can make doing that every day a reality."

His hands stilled. Mara felt him twitch within her. Her desire stirred again.

He raised a hand, settling it on the side of her head and raising her face so he could look at her. She smiled at him, not taking back the words. She wanted more of this. More of him. And that meant something about their relationship needed to change.

"What do you mean? How?"

"I think we need to talk about seeing each other more frequently. I know we have dinner or go do something together a couple times a week, but I—" Nerves hit her suddenly. Putting the thought into words was a lot different than just thinking it. "I think we need to spend our evenings together when you're not working. Either here or at your house. And on the days you have to work nights, maybe have lunch. Or breakfast. I want more than a couple dates a week."

His thumb stroked her cheekbone as he studied her, his face expressionless. Mara cursed his military and police training. She couldn't tell what he was thinking. The clamminess on her palms from earlier came back, but she refused to wipe it off. Partly because neither of them were wearing pants.

"I think I like that idea. There have been several nights where I wanted to come over and didn't. I didn't want to move things too fast. I know this is your first real relationship since your husband died, and I didn't want to pressure you into anything."

Warmth flooded Mara's veins at his thoughtfulness and made her heart swell. She framed his face in her hands and kissed him. Gentling her touch, she lifted her head. "Thank you. And just so you know, there's no need for you to feel like we're moving too fast. You've thoroughly blown past whatever reservations I had about being in a relationship again. I will always hold a special place in my heart for Blake, but I'm ready to move on. And that's because of you."

He tipped his chin forward and kissed her again, then groaned as he pulled back. "Now I really wish we hadn't committed to this dinner. I want to continue this"—he thrust his hips up, making Mara gasp—"in the bedroom. And I don't have hard and fast in me again just yet. It'd have to be long and slow."

She moaned and let her forehead rest against his. "Later. For sure." With one last roll of her hips, she rose, separating them. On shaky legs, she walked over to her panties and picked them up. From the corner of her eye, she watched him get up and grab his pants. It pained her to watch him cover up when all she wanted to do was strip everything off. Dinner would be quick, she vowed.

TWENTY-TWO

Carter rattled the change in his pocket as they waited to be seated at the restaurant. Despite their little interlude, they were the first ones to arrive.

The door opened behind him, and he glanced back to see Ben holding the door for Gemma. She saw him and waved, a pretty smile on her face.

He returned her smile and wave.

"Sorry we're a bit late. Meredith was a little fussy, and I didn't want to leave her until she settled," Gemma said. "Although, it looks like you just got here too."

Carter nodded.

"Do you know if Brooke and Johnathan are on their way?" Mara stepped up beside him.

"They're not coming." Gemma wrinkled her nose, annoyance on her face.

"What?" Mara glanced at Carter, then back to Gemma. "Why?"

"Johnathan had to go out of town at the last minute." Gemma rolled her eyes, her expression telling Carter she didn't buy that story.

"Didn't this happen to you guys one other time?" Mara asked.

"Yep." Gemma let the last letter pop. "I know she says she's happy, but sometimes I wonder if she's lying to herself. They never do anything she wants to do. Something always comes up."

Carter frowned, not liking the sound of that. "She's never shown signs of abuse, has she?"

"No. She can be deferential to him, but I don't think he's ever hit her. And she's not afraid of him. Right, Mara?" Gemma's gaze flicked to her friend.

Mara nodded. "I've actually only met him a few times, but they seemed like a normal couple. But I understand what you mean about the way she acts with him. She does tend to do what he wants. It's more like she's worried he'll leave, though, than because she's scared he'll hurt her later."

Carter glanced at Ben, whose face was carefully blank. That alone told Carter the man had his own opinions about Brooke's fiancé, but didn't want to rock the boat. Something about Johnathan likely bugged Ben, but it wasn't rooted in anything except a feeling. Carter vowed to pay attention when he met the man. He owed it to Brooke to make sure she was safe and happy. Without her, he wouldn't have Mara.

Ben broke eye contact with Carter and put a hand on his wife's back, ushering her closer to the hostess stand. "Come on. We can't do anything about Brooke and Johnathan right now. Let's enjoy our dinner."

Carter understood the implication in Ben's words. They'd make sure Brooke wasn't in any danger.

The hostess returned and motioned for them to follow her. She led them through the restaurant to a round booth in the corner. Carter waited for Mara to slide in, then sat down beside her. Ben did the same with Gemma on the other side.

The hostess handed them menus and took their drink orders, then left.

"What are you going to get?" Mara leaned into him, her voice soft.

"I was thinking one of their spicy sushi sampler entrees." He loved sushi, but only if it had a kick.

She wrinkled her nose. "You better brush your teeth and gargle with mouthwash before you kiss me."

He chuckled. "What don't you like? The spice or the sushi?"

"The seaweed. It just tastes like seawater, which is gross. I'll eat the unwrapped stuff, though."

"So, what are you going to get?"

"Probably the hibachi plate," she said with a chuckle.

Their server appeared with their drinks. Carter was about to ask the others if they were ready to order when his phone dinged with the alert tone for his new security system. He glanced at the young woman. "Can you give us a few minutes?"

She nodded and walked away as Carter opened his phone and clicked on the notification. His eyes went wide.

"What?" Ben's voice held a note of authority.

"Something's going on at my house. Maverick's going nuts in his kennel." He couldn't see the inside of the house, but he could hear the dog on the exterior camera. Opening the controls, he turned the camera on the corner of the house closest to the dog's kennel and pointed it toward the window. The curtain fluttered in the breeze through the broken window. "Shit. Someone broke the window."

Ben had his phone out in an instant and was on the line with dispatch to send a cruiser to his house.

"That doesn't sound right." Mara frowned, leaning closer.

A furrow formed between Carter's eyes. "It doesn't, no." Maverick's barks weren't what he would expect from someone breaking the window. Instead of deep and holding a note of warning, they were sharp and panicked. "Something's wrong." He looked up at Ben. "Tell them to step on it." He scooted toward the edge of the booth. "We need to go."

"Yep." Ben slid out his side, then held out a hand to Gemma.

Carter helped Mara from the booth, then took out his wallet and tossed a twenty on the table. On their way out the door, they passed their server, barely noting her look of confusion. His attention was on the video feed playing on his phone. Maverick had started to cough. Dread filled him, settling into a lead ball in his stomach. "Ben, I think someone threw tear gas or a smoke bomb into my house."

"What?" Ben cursed. "I'll call it in on the road. Are you good to drive?"

"Hell, yes." Let someone try to take his keys. They'd have to handcuff him and throw him in a cage.

Ben held his gaze for a moment, then nodded. "Just remember, you have precious cargo." He pointed at Mara.

"I know. I'm good, Ben. Can we stop jawing and go now?"

With a short nod, Ben pulled Gemma toward their vehicle. "I'll lead."

Grinding his teeth, but knowing it was probably best so he didn't speed too much, he nodded. He had no intention of putting himself or Mara in danger, but there was no doubt he would push the speedometer needle well past the speed limit.

Tugging on Mara's hand, they jogged toward his truck, and he helped her inside.

"Give me your phone." Mara held out her hand. "You can't drive and monitor it."

He handed it over, then rounded the hood to get in. The engine roared to life with a quick flick of his wrist. He buckled up and pulled out of the lot behind Ben.

"What do you see?" He glanced at the device in her hands,

but couldn't see anything from this distance. "Are those sirens?"

She nodded. A moment later, the sirens grew louder, filling the truck cab until she had to turn down the volume.

"Ben must have gotten through to dispatch. The officers are wearing gas masks."

Carter heard the officers' muffled voices as they announced themselves, then the distinctive tinkle of glass as they cleared the windowsill of glass shards so they could get inside.

Maverick's barks changed to a more threatening tone, even as he continued to cough. Carter drummed his fingers on the steering wheel. "This is not good. They need to get him out of the house, but they're likely to get bitten. Let me see your phone."

"My phone?"

"Yeah." Carter held out his hand.

Mara dug through her purse and lifted it free. Unlocking it, she laid it in his outstretched palm. Carter clicked on her phone app and called dispatch. After identifying himself, he asked to be patched through to the officers in his house. When the lead officer came on the line, Carter didn't waste time.

"There's a leash on a hook by the door to the garage. Put the clip through the handle and make a loop. One of you needs to distract him while the other gets the loop around his neck. You only need to control him well enough to get him out the back door into the yard. Don't go into the kennel with him unless you have the leash on. He's freaked out."

The officer's garbled affirmative came over the line, then it went silent as the man went to subdue Maverick. Carter edged the speedometer needle higher, riding Ben's bumper as he waited to hear if the officers were successful. Two minutes passed before the line crackled to life again.

"Remind me never to run from you," the officer said.

"He's a beast, even feeling the effects of the tear gas. But we got him into the yard without incident. My partner asked dispatch to get the vet over here. They'll be waiting for you."

Carter breathed a cautious sigh of relief. Maverick still needed treatment, but at least he was out of the gas. "Okay. Thank you. ETA is about fifteen minutes." And it would be some of the longest minutes of Carter's life. He hung up the phone and handed it back to Mara. "Can you switch to the cameras on the back of the house?"

She nodded and touched the screen.

"How's he look?"

"Miserable. He's pawing at his face and rolling in the grass." Her voice was tight as she relayed what she saw.

Carter slammed a hand on the steering wheel. "Dammit!" He growled and gripped the wheel, his knuckles turning white. "Go to the stored footage and look at the front cameras. See if we caught this bastard on video."

Mara thumbed through the controls, doing as he asked.

"Anything?"

"Not yet. No, wait." She sat up, touching the screen.

Carter glanced over, but still couldn't see anything.

She growled. "Oh, this person's smart. They put on a ball cap and pulled it low, then raised their hood. I can't see their face. But—" She tipped her head, staring at the screen. "I think it's a woman."

An image of Amy Spalding popped into his head. And so did the details from the break-in at the equestrian center. That figure looked like a woman too. Maybe the incident there was connected to the ones at his house. But why? If it was Amy, what reason could she have for destroying the center's feed stores? It didn't make any sense.

Grinding his molars, Carter willed Ben to drive faster, but the sheriff kept the same steady pace. When they finally turned into his neighborhood, Carter buzzed with pent up energy and frustration. He parked as close as he could get to the scene, then flew out of the car, calling for Mara to stay with Gemma.

"Dispatch filled me in," Ben said, coming up beside Carter as they ran toward the rear of the house. "Good call on getting patched into the officers on-scene."

"But you still didn't drive any faster," Carter growled.

"I went as fast as was safe, you know that. We weren't in vehicles equipped with lights and sirens."

With a grunt, Carter reached for the gate latch. He was sure he'd agree with Ben later, but not right now. Pushing open the gate, he stepped into the yard. Maverick rolled in the grass still, soft whimpers and whines floating on the chilly breeze.

Anger surged again, even as his heart bled for the dog. "Maverick, *hier*." He called the dog, hoping his voice was enough to break past the animal's pain.

Maverick rolled to his feet, his head turning toward Carter's voice. Even in the low light, Carter could tell the dog's eyes were swollen. He glanced at Ben. "Get the vet back here. And get me some water." He ran toward his dog as Ben lifted the handheld radio he'd brought from his car. Carter repeated the command for Maverick to come. He was met with a whine before the animal flopped back into the grass and rolled again.

"Don't touch him," Ben yelled, running up. "You'll get it on you and then I'll have to call medical for your ass." He held out a pair of winter gloves.

"Thanks." Carter put them on, then dropped to his knees beside Maverick. "Oh, buddy. I'm so sorry."

"Vet's coming," Ben said. "She's getting her gear. I've got an officer raiding your kitchen for bottled water."

No sooner were the words out of his mouth than the back door opened and an officer in a gas mask stepped out, holding several water bottles. He whipped off his mask and loped toward Carter.

"Here." He held out the water. "There's still more inside if you need it."

Carter cracked one open and poured it over Mav's face. The dog twisted, trying to get away, then paused as he realized the water helped.

"That's a good boy." Carter emptied the bottle and grabbed another. Commotion at the gate drew his attention. He looked over to see the vet, Kay Morris, hurry through. Gemma and Mara followed. He frowned as they approached, his gaze on Mara. "You were supposed to stay in the truck."

"No. You told me to stay with Gemma. She decided to follow the vet." She shrugged. "I did what you said. How is he?" She pointed at the dog.

Carter's mouth flattened, but he didn't argue. He glanced at Maverick, who was now drenched and still coughing.

The vet dropped to her knees beside the dog. "Carter, go get your hose. We need to wash him off."

"In the cold?"

"Yes. The cold will actually help. It'll close off his pores. Go." She shooed him with one hand.

He stood and ran toward the house, pulling his hose out of its housing and turning on the spigot, glad he forgot to shut off the valve inside this winter. With the end of the hose in hand, he ran back to Maverick.

"Drench him," Kay ordered.

Carter set the nozzle to full and squeezed the handle. The dog skirted to the side as the icy blast of water hit him. Calling him back, Carter held the scruff of his neck with one hand while he sprayed him with the other. Kay ran her gloved hands through his fur, making sure the water made it all the way to his skin. By the time she was satisfied, they were all shivering. Ben asked an officer to bring them some blankets, and Carter used one to dry the dog, then another to wrap Maverick up as he lifted him to carry him to the car. The dog still coughed and had started to wheeze.

Mara ran ahead and opened the rear passenger door. Carter stepped inside, laying the dog on the seat.

"Meet me at my clinic," Kay yelled as she passed.

Carter waved in acknowledgment.

"You stay there. I'll drive." Mara shut the door before he could reply, but he didn't mind. He'd be too distracted, worrying about Mav alone in the backseat to focus on the road.

"Do you know where you're going?"

She shook her head as she fastened her seat belt and started the engine. "No, but I'm just following the vet." She pointed out the windshield.

"Holler if you lose her, and I'll get you there."

"Yep."

He shifted forward as she put the truck in gear and pulled away from the curb. Bracing himself, he stroked a hand through Maverick's wet fur, trying to calm the animal. He could tell from the dog's wide-eyed look he was still scared. Carter would be too if he struggled to take a breath without coughing or wheezing. He was scared for him.

Rubbing his temple, Carter said a silent prayer Mav would be all right. He couldn't lose him. Not like this.

TWENTY-THREE

Mara stood in the doorway to the kennels at the vet's office, watching as Carter gave Maverick's head one last stroke before rising and backing out of the cage. The dog didn't move, too worn out from his ordeal to care that he was somewhere foreign.

Metal clinked as Carter shut the door and latched it. When he turned and headed toward her, Mara sucked her bottom lip between her teeth and bit down to hold back the tears pressing against the backs of her eyes. His weary, dejected expression tore at her heart. She could tell he didn't want to leave the dog, but there was nothing more he could do here tonight. Maverick would be okay, and they all needed to get some rest.

Without a word, Mara took his hand. Squeezing it, she offered him a tremulous smile, then turned and headed for the exit. Cold night air blasted them in the face as they pushed through the door. She was glad she'd started the truck a few minutes ago. Carter was still damp and had to be freezing.

She unlocked the doors and climbed into the driver's seat.

He got in beside her and quickly pointed the air vents at himself and turned on the seat warmer.

"Where do you want me to take you?" Mara turned in her seat to look at him. "You can't go back to your house. Do you want to come home with me?"

He scrubbed a hand over his face. "Can you run me to the station first? I have a change of clothes in my locker."

"Sure." Mara clicked her seat belt into place, then put the truck in gear, heading for the sheriff's department.

Silence reigned in the cab as she drove, but it wasn't uncomfortable. After the craziness of the last couple of hours, they both needed to process things.

She pulled into the lot at the station and parked near the rear entrance.

"Do you want to wait out here or come inside?" Carter glanced at her, one hand on the door latch. "I might be a bit. I want to talk to Ben." He pointed at the black SUV parked two spaces over.

"I'll come inside, then, if you don't mind? I'd like to hear what he has to say too."

Carter nodded and pulled on the door handle. Mara followed him from the truck and into the building. They stopped long enough to get her a visitor's badge, then he led her down a long hallway to the ready room.

"I'm going to run in and change." He pointed to the locker room door marked *Men*. "You can hang out in here." He gestured to the couches in the common area. "I won't be long."

Mara nodded and wandered over to sit down as he disappeared through the doorway. She glanced around, taking in the basic, office-style décor. A small kitchenette took up one corner, the smell of stale, burnt coffee wafting her way from its direction. She hated that smell. It reminded her of the hospital consultation area she'd been sequestered in just before the doctor came in to tell her Blake had died.

Getting up, she paced to the door and glanced through the window inset into the wood. The station was quiet at this hour, so there was little to see.

The door behind her swished open, and she turned to see Carter walk through, dressed in black tactical pants and a department t-shirt. He held his balled-up soggy clothes in one hand and carried his coat in the other.

"Better?" she asked, raising an eyebrow.

"Much. Let's go find Ben." He walked toward her and pushed the door open.

They wandered further down the hall and made a turn before he stopped in front of Ben's office. When they peered in, Ben looked up.

"Hey." The pensive expression turning his brows down lifted. "How's Maverick?"

"Exhausted. But he should be fine. Kay put him on oxygen and gave him an antidote to the tear gas. He was resting when we left. We'll know if there were any permanent effects in the next couple of days." Carter tucked his clothes under his arm and stuffed his hands in his pockets, his muscles tense.

Mara curled her hands into fists to keep from reaching out. Everything about his posture screamed that he was walling himself off so he could hold it together. She didn't want to do anything to undo him here. He could fall apart later, when they were alone.

Ben blew out a breath. "Good. Hopefully, he'll make a complete recovery. He only spent about five minutes in the gas. I looked it up. It's not lethal to a dog his size until after about thirty minutes."

"Yeah. I'm just thankful we got that camera system up when we did. We wouldn't have known about it until it was too late."

His voice cracked, and Mara couldn't stop herself. She darted a hand out and wrapped it around his arm. He took his hand from his pocket and laced their fingers, then squeezed, the grip just shy of painful.

Carter cleared his throat. "Did the video reveal any more?"

"Actually, yes. It caught a car driving past at a high rate of speed not long after the hooded figure ran off. We weren't lucky enough to catch a license plate, but the car was a light-colored mid-size SUV."

A new sort of tension filled Carter's muscles, and his grip on Mara's hand loosened as he rocked slightly forward on the balls of his feet. "Could you tell make and model?"

Ben nodded and gave them the information. "I've got deputies on the lookout for it. So does the city. I forwarded the information to Agent Porter as well. We'll find them."

Mara felt the anxious energy humming through Carter's body. He wanted to go look for the car.

Ben's gaze narrowed as he stared at Carter. "Go home. Get some rest. That's what I plan to do soon too. The guys know to call you if they bring someone in."

"He's right." Mara tugged on his hand. "Let your colleagues do their jobs."

"Besides," Ben chimed in. "You can't be anywhere near the arrest. It's best if you go home."

Carter snorted. "It might be best, but it doesn't change my desire to go find the person responsible." He shook his head. "But you're right. I don't want them to walk because I got involved. Tell them to look at Amy Spalding. She threatened to come after me and Mav after I arrested her husband for felony drug possession. Of all the people I looked at, she stuck out the most."

Ben nodded. "Will do."

Carter took a step back, tugging on Mara's hand. "We'll be at Mara's. I can't go home until I get my house cleaned."

Ben nodded. "Okay, I'll text you the number for the restoration cleaners. You can call them in the morning."

"Sounds good. Thanks, Ben."

"Yep." He made a shooing motion. "Get out of here, so I can finish up and go home myself."

A smile tugged on one corner of Carter's mouth. "Yes, sir."

Mara waggled her fingers at Ben, and they left. Passing through the building, they stopped long enough to turn her badge in, then headed for his truck. Once inside, Mara pointed the vehicle toward her house for the short ride home.

"You okay?" She glanced over, taking in his tense posture. He drummed his fingers on his knee and stared straight ahead.

"I'm fine." He didn't look at her.

Mara scoffed. "Yeah, okay."

Carter sighed, and his fingers stopped their tattoo on his leg. "I'm fine enough. How's that?"

"Better." She offered him a soft smile.

This time, he looked at her. His features softened. "Thank you."

A frown wrinkled her forehead. "For what?"

"For being here. For doing what was needed without question. For keeping me from running off and doing something dumb. I know you didn't jump into the driver's seat just now to keep me from going out to look for that car, but if you weren't here, I might have done just that, consequences be damned."

Mara patted his knee, then wrapped her fingers around his hand. "You might have, yes. But you're smart enough to realize you'd need someone else to make the arrest and would have called for backup."

He quirked one eyebrow and tipped his head. "Maybe." His gaze returned to the windshield, and he shook his head. "It's been a long time since something made me this angry.

They want to target me? Fine. But leave my dog—and you—out of it."

She'd prefer they left him out of it too. She wasn't sure she'd make it through losing another man she loved.

Her eyes widened as that thought ran through her head, and she turned her face away so Carter couldn't read her thoughts. Did she really just think that? Her mind spun as she analyzed her feelings behind her thoughts. She wanted to deny it—it was too soon for her to be in love with him. Never mind that she knew she was falling in love. That was completely different from *being* in love. Falling in love took time. She spent months falling in love with Blake. It hadn't even been three weeks since her first date with Carter.

But she couldn't deny what was in her heart. She'd fallen for the quiet deputy. His steadfast, loyal nature and quick, charming smile blasted past the walls she'd erected after Blake's death. Her heart knew it had found someone who would take care to consider her feelings and treat her with love, respect, and patience. He would bend over backward to ensure her happiness. And she wanted to do the same for him. She wanted to be his rock in the storm. Just as much as she was sure he'd be hers.

"Sorry. I didn't mean to shock you."

"What?" Mara glanced at him. Could he tell what she was thinking? Because her revelation had sure as hell shocked her.

"What I said. You got quiet. I didn't mean to shock you with it. I can be a little unforgiving when someone threatens those I care about, and it makes it hard to keep my emotions in check. I got a little more vehement than I intended."

"Oh. That. No, you're fine. I'd probably say the same thing if the situation were reversed."

At his silence, she chanced a glance at him. He watched her with a curious frown.

"Then what's bothering you?"

"What?" She needed to stop saying that, or he'd never believe that she was right as rain and her world hadn't shifted on its axis. "Nothing's bothering me. I'm just tired." Which was half the reason she was having trouble keeping her emotions off her face.

He hummed, clearly not believing her. Mara kept her eyes on the road. Luckily, they were entering her neighborhood. She turned onto her street, then into her driveway a moment later, negating any chance at continuing the conversation.

Parking his truck in front of her garage, she shut it off and climbed out, hurrying through the cold to her front door. Mara fumbled with her keys to find the correct one, then thrust it in the lock and let them into the house. She did a little shake, ridding herself of the chill from outside. "I am ready for a hot shower and bed."

Carter took off his coat and hung it up, rolling his shoulders. "A hot shower sounds great. Maybe it'll help relax me. Right now, I feel like I'll never fall asleep."

"Why don't you go shower? I need to go dig my pajamas out of the dryer." That wasn't a lie. She'd washed them this morning. But she had others she could wear. What she really needed, though, was to have a little space.

He raised an eyebrow at her, his intelligence shining from his eyes. Mara knew he was perplexed by her behavior, but she prayed he'd let it go and give her some space to think.

After a long moment, he nodded, then retreated down the hallway to her bedroom.

She let out a long sigh and covered her face with her hands. How was she going to keep herself from telling him how she felt? Should she? They'd both agreed this was going somewhere. But it was so fast.

Groaning, she dropped her hands and spun, heading for her laundry room. She needed to quit worrying about it tonight. Tomorrow, when she was more rested and thinking more clearly, she'd figure out what to do. But for now, she was taking a shower and snuggling into his arms to sleep. She'd sort out her life in the daylight.

TWENTY-FOUR

Stinger's hooves thundered over the ground as Mara put him through his paces. Leaning low in the saddle, she squeezed her thighs to stay astride him as he looped around the final barrel and headed for the fence. They crossed the imaginary finish line she drew in the dirt, and she pulled back on the reins, bringing him down to a walk. The horse tossed his head, wanting to go again. Mara would love to, but she had a meeting to get to.

She was looking forward to this one. Most meetings bored her to tears, but this one was with a potential donor. The news media caught wind of the vandalism and ran a story on it. Yesterday, a woman contacted her about making a rather large donation to the equestrian center, but she wanted to meet with Mara to discuss the particulars.

Opening the gate, Mara rode through, then shut it before turning Stinger toward the stables. His hooves clopped on the concrete floor, and he let out a whicker as he realized their ride was over. She patted his neck. "Sorry, boy. One day soon, we'll go for a long ride. I still need to get Carter on a horse."

At his stall, she hopped off and led him inside, removing

his tack and brushing him down. Once she checked his hay bag and water bucket, she put her saddle and bridle away, then headed back to her office. The woman—Constance Miller—would arrive any time now.

Sitting down in her chair, Mara tugged off her riding boots and set them behind her, then slid her feet into her flats. She wiggled her toes and grimaced as the heel bit into her foot. She'd much rather stay in her boots.

The desk phone beeped, and Mara picked it up.

"Mara, your appointment is here." Pam's cheery voice came over the line.

"Great. Send her in. Thanks, Pam."

"You're welcome. She'll be down in a moment."

Mara hung up and stood, rounding her desk to open her door. She glanced into the hall to see a slender blonde woman about her height coming her way. Dressed in flowy gray trousers and a salmon-colored sweater with black ankle boots, the woman oozed confidence.

Smiling, Mara stepped into the hall and held out a hand. "Hello. Ms. Miller?"

The woman took Mara's hand and nodded, a polite smile on her face. "Yes."

"It's nice to meet you. I'm Mara Roth. Come in, please." She released Ms. Miller's hand and turned, walking into her office. "Have a seat." She motioned to the guest chair as she walked around her desk.

"Thank you." The woman sank into the chair and set her handbag on the floor.

Mara sat down and folded her hands on the desk.

"I appreciate you taking the time to meet with me. I didn't want to write such a large check without seeing your operation first." Constance's gaze traveled around the room.

"I completely understand. I'm happy I could accommodate your schedule. What would you like to do first? Go over the business side of our operation or see it in action?"

"Since we're in here, why don't we go over the business side first?"

"Of course." Mara sat up and reached for the press kit she kept handy for all potential donors. "So, you were a little vague on the phone. What made you want to donate to us?"

"My husband loved to ride. I've been struggling with what to do with his life insurance money since he passed away several years ago. We didn't have any children. We were only married less than a year when he died."

"Oh." Mara's heart lurched. "I'm so sorry. I lost my husband too. Three years ago, to a car accident. I know how you feel."

Ms. Miller took a tissue from the box on Mara's desk and dabbed at the corner of her eye. "I'm sorry." She offered Mara a rueful smile. "I told myself doing this wouldn't make me cry. Kyle's been gone a long time. But it's hard, though, you know? Little things make me think of him."

Mara nodded. She knew exactly what the woman meant.

"Anyway," Constance waved a hand. "Enough of my melancholy. Show me what you've got."

"Of course." Mara opened the folder and turned it so Ms. Miller could see, then went over the information inside. The woman asked several pertinent questions before they were finished.

"Your program sounds wonderful. I think I'd like that tour now."

"Certainly." Mara stood and led her down the hall to the arena and stables. They wandered through the facility while Mara pointed out different things and told her about the classes they conducted and the types of therapy they offered. Once they finished the tour, they returned to Mara's office.

"I must say, I'm impressed with this facility. It's clean,

well-run, and both riders and horses seem like they're having a good time. Kyle would approve."

"Thank you, Ms. Miller."

"Call me Constance, please." She sat down in the guest chair and picked up her purse, opening it to rummage inside. She pulled out a checkbook.

"Wait. You're writing the check now?" Mara frowned. Most donations of her size came through an attorney's office and there was pomp and circumstance involved.

Constance's brow furrowed. "Well, yes. Why wouldn't I?"

Mara rounded her desk and sat down. "We usually do some sort of media op. You know, we invite some reporters who take pictures and then write up a story, showing everyone your generosity."

"Oh, I don't need any of that. If you want to put Kyle's name on a plaque and hang it up, that would be fine, but there's no need for any grand gesture."

"Are you sure?"

"Completely." Constance plucked a pen from the cup on Mara's desk. "Now, who do I make this out to?"

Flabbergasted, Mara named the equestrian center. Constance scrolled the information across the check face— along with an eye-popping sum—then tore the check out and handed it to her.

"Thank you so much for your generosity, Ms. Miller. We'll definitely get that plaque made, honoring his memory. Would you like to have a ceremony for that?"

Constance pursed her lips. "Maybe."

"Well, how about I call you when it comes in, and we'll decide then?"

"That sounds good." She stuffed her checkbook into her purse and rose. "It was a pleasure to meet you. I trust you'll put the funds to good use." She held out a hand.

Mara stood, a bit confused by the woman's abrupt departure. She shook Constance's hand. "Of course. I'll be sure to let you know how we use it."

"Great." Constance released Mara's hand. "I look forward to seeing that plaque." With a wave of her fingers, she exited the office.

A little out of sorts, Mara stared after her. That was weird. She glanced down at the check. Really weird. No one had ever handed her a check for a hundred grand with such indifference. Like it didn't matter. Even Brooke, who threw around cash like it was notebook paper, showed more regard for how she spent her money than Constance Miller.

Footsteps approaching drew her attention. The accompanied click-clack of toenails clued her in to who it was a moment before Carter and Maverick appeared in her doorway. Smile blooming, she set the check down and hurried around the front of her desk to drop down in front of the dog. "Hey, buddy." She buried her fingers in his soft fur and scratched. Maverick's tongue lolled out, and he tipped his head. "How are you doing?"

"He's right as rain," Carter said with a smile. "His stomach is still a little off, but the vet said it's nothing that won't correct itself in the next day or so."

"That's great." She leaned in and hugged the dog, then kissed his head. "I'm glad you're okay."

Maverick pressed his nose to her cheek, then tipped his head into her hand.

Mara laughed and scratched his ears again.

"Who was that woman who just left?"

"Huh?" Mara glanced up, forehead wrinkling as she switched gears. "Blonde? About my height?"

He nodded. "She gave me a look. Stared right at me, like she knew me and disapproved."

Mara's frown deepened. "Hmm, strange. Her name's

Constance Miller. She just donated a hundred thousand dollars to the center."

Carter's mouth dropped open, and his eyes rounded. "What?"

"I know. Shocked the crap out of me too. She saw the story on the news about the break-in and called yesterday, wanting to meet with me about a possible donation. Today, she told me the money was from her husband's life insurance. He died several years ago and loved horses. She thought he'd approve of her donating the money to us."

"Why wouldn't she keep it?"

Mara shrugged and stood. "She said they hadn't been married long when he died, and that they didn't have any kids. I guess she wanted to do something valuable with it instead of just letting it languish in the bank."

"And she just wrote you a check?"

"Yep."

"For a hundred grand?"

She nodded.

"Let me see the check."

Mara turned and took two steps to her desk, leaning over to pick it up. She handed it to him.

Carter turned the paper over in his hands, then held it up to the light. "It looks legit."

Her lips twitched. "You think too much like a cop all the time. Why can't she just want to do something good with her money?"

His mouth flattened, and he handed her back the check. "Because people with a hundred thousand dollars to spend don't just drop out of the sky. You said her name is Constance Miller?"

"Yes. Why?"

"Let me do some digging on her before you cash that. Just in case this is some sort of scam."

"Why would she give me a check to cash if she was scamming me?"

"If you deposit that and spend it before the bank verifies its validity, you're on the hook for the money. You'll see it approved in your bank account long before they actually verify it."

"Well, that's just mean. Why would she do something like that?" She propped her hands on her hips and frowned.

"You didn't see the look she gave me, Mara. I'm telling you, don't cash that check yet."

Mara sighed. "Fine."

"What else did she tell you about herself?"

"Just her husband's name. Kyle. I'm not sure where she lives. Around here, somewhere, since she saw the story on the news."

Carter's brows dipped, and he nodded. "I'll see what I can find out."

"Sounds good." She ran a hand through her hair. Well, that was a bummer. She'd been riding high. Now her enthusiasm was tempered with a dose of reality. Carter was right. She needed to know more about Constance Miller and should have done her homework before accepting that check. She'd been blinded by the zeros.

Pushing those thoughts away for now, she looked at Maverick, then back to Carter. "So, did you stop by to show me Maverick had been released, or did you have another motive?"

"Lunch." He chuckled as she grinned. "Mostly, though, it was to show you Mav was home. I also got someone to clean my house. They're coming tomorrow." His smile dimmed.

Mara gave him a curious look. "Why do you sound upset about that?"

"Because I've liked spending all this time with you. It's nice waking up to you. Coming home to you." He reached out and traced her cheekbone with his knuckles. "I know we sort of talked about making more time for each other, but I think we need to sit down and really talk about how to make that a reality. I don't want to go back to the way things were."

She sucked in a breath and trapped her bottom lip between her teeth, worrying it for a moment before setting it free. The words singing in her heart pushed their way up her throat, but she swallowed them back. He wanted to take them to a higher level, but she didn't think he meant that high. So, she'd wait. Until she knew he could say it back. She wasn't sure she could take it if she told him she loved him and he didn't feel the same way. Even if he told her he was on that road, it would still hurt to know he didn't love her yet. Instead, she nodded. "I don't, either."

His expression morphed into a bright smile. "Good. How about we go grab some lunch and talk about it?"

Mara scrunched up her face. "Sorry. I can't."

His smile fell.

"I wish I could," she hastened to add. "But I've only got about fifteen minutes until my next session. I squeezed Ms. Miller into my lunch break."

"Well, that sucks."

Mara giggled. "I know. I'm sorry. How about we cook dinner together tonight? We can talk then."

His smile returned, and he leaned down. "That sounds perfect." He kissed her, lingering for a long moment. "I'll see you in a few hours."

He'd stolen her breath with the tender kiss, so she just nodded.

With a wave, he gave Maverick a quick command to heel, and they left.

Mara closed her door and leaned against it. Anticipation, along with a healthy dose of nerves, filled her. How could she be in love, but nervous to move in with the man?

Twenty-Five

Carter moved through his house wearing a gas mask and carrying a trash bag. He wanted to take a load of clothes out and wash them. He'd already grabbed a few things, but it would take time to wash everything. The likelihood they were contaminated was low, since most stuff was in his dresser or closet and the gas had been in the living room, but he wasn't taking any chances. Maverick's reaction had been severe, and Carter didn't want to give the dog issues because the residue remained on his clothing.

Heading for his closet, he filled the bag with an assortment of casual clothes and uniforms. Tying it shut, he went outside to his cruiser. Fresh air hit his face as he took off the mask. The bite of cold felt good after being in the stuffy mask.

Maverick barked as he approached the car, objecting to being left in the vehicle while he went inside. This was home, and the dog knew it.

Carter opened the tailgate and peered through to the backseat. Maverick barked again. "Sorry, buddy." He took the lid off the plastic tote in the back and put the bag inside. Closing it up, he shut the hatch, then got in the car.

Mav stuck his head through the door in the steel wall separating his kennel from the front seat. He bumped Carter's shoulder with his nose and let out a sharp yip.

"I know, I know. But we can't go home yet. We're going to Mara's instead, okay?" His plan was to drop the clothes off and start a load of laundry, then reassemble Maverick's indoor kennel. He'd picked it up before he picked the dog up from the vet, knowing he still couldn't inhabit his house.

After the conversation he had with Mara a little while ago, he couldn't help but wonder if it would ever go back into his house. The last couple of days with her had been amazing. He knew it was early, and the situation was new, but living under the same roof felt right.

But he also couldn't lie and say he wasn't terrified. Their relationship was a whirlwind. The feelings that had developed between them were so strong and came up so fast it had been hard not to be caught up in the swell. He just hoped they didn't crash and get destroyed when they came down from the top. If they wanted this to work, they needed to figure out how to steer this ship.

Carter turned his cruiser into Mara's neighborhood and backed into her driveway. He would need to move before she got home so she could get into her garage. If they decided to move in together, they needed to really think about whose house they were living in. Mara's was nicer, but she only had a one-car garage. And no fence. The fence he could fix, but not the garage situation. At least not easily. There was enough room on her property for them to build a bigger garage, but would it be worth the hassle when his house already had enough space for all their vehicles?

Climbing out, he let Maverick out of the car, commanding him to heel, then grabbed the bag of clothes from the back and went inside. Maverick ran off to sniff his new surroundings while Carter wandered to the laundry tucked into Mara's bathroom. Starting the washer, he returned to the living room and stared at the pieces of kennel leaning against the wall. With a sigh, he found a screwdriver in a junk drawer in the kitchen and got to work.

The kennel wasn't hard to assemble, just awkward and time-consuming. Once he had it together, he fetched Maverick's bedding from the dryer and switched his clothes over before starting another load. Finished with his chores for now, he glanced at Maverick, who'd followed him. "What do you think we should do now?"

The dog tipped his head, then barked.

"I think you're right. A long walk sounds nice." He didn't want to tax the dog's lungs too much yet with a run, but he could handle a walk. They could wander down to the station where he could run the name of that woman who donated to the equestrian center. "Come on." Motioning for the animal to follow and repeating the command in German, he led Maverick to the kitchen, where he'd hung his harness and leash. Once the dog was ready, he locked the house and left.

Foggy Mountain wasn't a large city. Mara's house was about a mile from the sheriff's office, which made for a decent walk for the recovering Malinois.

Warm air blasted Carter in the face as he let them into the station.

"Hey, Townsend."

Carter paused as Jake Maxwell greeted him. "Hi, Jake."

"How's Maverick?" The younger man motioned to the dog, who stood next to Carter, his tongue lolling out of his mouth.

"He's doing well. Should be back on patrol by the end of the week."

"Glad to hear it."

"Me too. Hey, did you get any more on who threw the tear gas into my house?"

Jake's mouth flattened, and he shook his head. "No. We've got a BOLO out on the car, but it's a pretty common make and model. We can't pull them all over."

"No. What about that woman I mentioned to Ben. Amy Spalding."

"She had a solid alibi. She was at work. Dozens of people saw her."

Carter bit the corner of his mouth, then nodded. "Okay. Well, keep me posted, yeah?"

"Of course."

With a nod, Carter walked away, heading for his desk, feeling a little dejected. She'd been his best suspect. Releasing a breath, he sat down. Maverick curled up into his bed at the end, and Carter logged into the system. He ran Constance Miller's name and came up with several hits. He used her husband's name to narrow the search. When he did that, he got zero results. Frowning, he widened the search to neighboring states, and still came up empty.

"Okay, fine. Let's see if there's a record of the husband's death," he muttered. Guessing at the age range, he input the husband's name and went back five years. There were several Kyle Millers, but none had a wife named Constance. He searched again, going back another five years, but still found nothing; not even when he widened the age range.

Tapping his fingers on his desk, Carter stared at the screen. He knew there was something off with that woman. Had she given Mara a false name? But why? What was her aim in scamming the equestrian center? None of the money Mara spent would go back to her; it would all go to the bank. All she'd succeed in doing was hurt the center's credit rating and put them in a financial bind.

"Damn."

Maverick raised his head at Carter's exclamation.

"I was hoping she was on the up and up for the center's

sake," he told the dog. Logging off, he pushed away from his desk. He told Maverick to stay, then went to Ben's office.

The sheriff looked up when Carter rapped his knuckles on the doorframe.

"Hey, Carter."

"Hey. Got a minute?"

Ben groaned. "I'm not going to like this, am I? I can see it on your face."

Carter grimaced. "Probably not."

"Come in." Ben motioned him inside. "What's up?"

Quickly, Carter relayed his concern with the equestrian center's newest donor, and the background search he ran. Ben's frown deepened with each word.

"I guess my biggest concern is I can't verify her identity. I don't want Mara cashing a check that large if we don't know who it came from."

"I agree. Did you get the woman's phone number?"

"No. I thought I had enough to go on with her name and her husband's name. Her number was my next step. If we can't verify who she is with that, then I want to open an official investigation and run the check she wrote."

Ben gave a short nod. "Sounds good. Keep me posted."

"Will do." Carter nodded, but made no move to rise. Another thought—one that had been swirling through his head for a while—kept him in his seat.

"You got something else on your mind?" Ben raised an eyebrow.

"Yeah." Carter glanced at the wall behind Ben, trying to put his spinning thoughts into words. "Do you get the feeling there's something bigger going on?"

"With the donor?"

"Not just her, but with all the trouble surrounding Mara and me lately. I feel like we're being targeted. I just don't know why. Or who could be doing it."

Ben leaned forward, crossing his arms on the desk. "When you put all the incidents together, yeah, it certainly seems like someone's targeting you. Or her."

"Maybe I should dig into my own past more." Perhaps take a deeper look at the people who jumped out at him the first time.

"Tristan and Jake are on that. They're tearing your professional life apart. What about Mara?"

"Mara? What about her?"

"She have any skeletons in her closet?"

It was Carter's turn to frown. "Not that I know of. But that's absurd. She's one of the nicest people I've ever met."

A mirthless smile crossed Ben's face. "This is why cops don't investigate loved ones. You're biased. Mara's only lived here a few years. Maybe something followed her."

"Like what? Her husband died in a car crash. She worked as an equestrian therapist in Oklahoma too. It's not like there's anything illicit in her past."

"That she's told you about."

Carter scoffed. "Why would the equestrian center here hire her as their director if she had problems in Oklahoma?"

"Maybe she lied."

The frown on Carter's faced turned into a scowl as anger swelled.

Ben held up a hand. "I'm just playing devil's advocate. I highly doubt she's ever been involved in anything nefarious. Mara's as sweet as they come. But it's my job—and yours—to look at things from every angle."

Carter blew out a breath, his anger fading. He ran a hand through his hair. "Yeah. Okay."

"Look, go home. Talk to her tonight. See if she can think of anyone who would want to cause her harm. And get the other information about that woman so we can run it."

Mouth flat, Carter nodded, then rose. With little more

than a quick wave, he exited Ben's office. Crossing the bullpen, he called to Maverick. The dog trotted to his side. Carter picked up his leash, and they left the station.

The day outside had warmed up, but Carter didn't feel the sunshine on his face. His thoughts were a jumble of questions and what-ifs. The incidents involving Mara didn't seem connected to the ones involving him, but he couldn't shake the feeling they were. And whatever was going on, he was certain he was the center of it. It didn't matter what Ben said. Carter didn't believe for a second that this was about Mara.

And that really just left him with one looming question: what was he supposed to do about it to keep her safe?

TWENTY-SIX

A quick thrill went up Mara's spine and made her heart skip as she turned onto her street and saw both Carter's truck and his cruiser parked out front of her house. There was no mistaking he was there. She was eager to see him. Since his visit earlier, she was distracted the rest of the day, excited to discuss their relationship.

She couldn't believe how much she was looking forward to taking the next step with him. With as hard as she'd fought not to date again, it should have been harder for her to commit to a man. But it wasn't. Things with Carter just felt right. Natural. It had all been going so well, it actually made her a bit leery. She kept waiting for the other shoe to drop. Surely, finding love again couldn't be this easy. There had to be some hiccup, some skeleton that would come to light and cast a shadow over their happiness. Right?

Mara turned into her drive and pushed the button above her rearview mirror to raise the garage door. She drove into the garage and parked, cutting the engine. Silence enveloped her, but her thoughts still raged. She sighed and picked up her purse. Whatever happened, she was going to enjoy what they had now. If Blake's death taught her anything, it was that life was short and never guaranteed.

Getting out of her car, she went inside, hitting the button on the interior garage wall to close the overhead door as she went. Stepping over the threshold, she smiled at Carter, who was in the kitchen. "Hey."

He looked up from chopping a green pepper and smiled. "Hey, yourself. How was the rest of your day?"

"Uneventful. Yours?"

A look she couldn't decipher crossed his face, but it quickly cleared, and he shrugged one shoulder. "The same."

Mara set her purse down on a dining chair and took off her coat, hanging it on a hook by the door. "I thought we were making dinner together. It looks like you've got it all handled."

"Not quite. I figured I'd chop up the vegetables now and just get a head start."

"What are they for?"

"Steak sandwiches."

"Oh, yum." Her mouth watered just thinking about it. "What do you want me to do?"

"You can start frying stuff. I'm about done chopping these peppers."

"Sounds good." Mara turned to the cabinet where she kept her pots and pans and took out a large skillet. She set it on the stove and added some butter before turning on the burner. Grabbing the bowl of chopped onion, she dumped it in the pan once the butter melted. Her stomach growled. It smelled divine.

Side by side, they made dinner. Their conversation stayed light, and they avoided the topic of their relationship for now. When the food was done, they plated everything and carried it to the table.

Mara lifted her sandwich and took a bite. Flavors burst over her tongue, and she held back a moan of delight. The food was good, but she'd been hungry too. Hungrier than she thought.

The light conversation continued until they finished eating. After carrying their plates to the dishwasher, they retreated to the living room. Mara tucked herself into the corner of the couch. Carter sat down next to her, and an awkwardness filled the room.

Her heart skipped a beat at the hesitation on his face. Why did he look so reluctant to talk? Did he have something else on his mind besides what they'd implied earlier?

"So, I've been giving what we talked about at lunchtime a lot of thought."

She hummed a non-answer, wanting him to continue. At least he hadn't kept her wondering long what that look was all about.

"I really like the idea of us making this"—he swirled a finger and glanced around the room—"more permanent."

A smile started on her face.

"But—" He broke off and glanced away.

Mara's smile died with that one word. "But what?"

His silvery eyes met hers. "Until we figure out what's going on with the vandalism and now with your mystery donor, I think we should slow things down."

A wrinkle formed between her eyes. "What? What does that mean?"

"It means that once my house is clean tomorrow, Maverick and I are moving back in. And we should probably limit our contact to phone calls and texts."

The wrinkle smoothed out as her eyebrows shot up. "You don't want to see me anymore?"

"No. Yes! Dammit!" He stood up and paced to the window, staring out at the street.

Mara's gaze followed him, taking note of the rigidity to his shoulders. His spine was ramrod-straight. When he turned to look at her again, his jaw was like granite, and there was a flintiness in his gray eyes she hadn't seen before. He'd closed himself off from her.

"Whatever is going on—it's about me. And it's putting you in danger. I probably shouldn't even be here now. Until we figure out what's going on—who's behind all this—you need to distance yourself from me."

Concern and anger warred within Mara's chest. She'd wondered, too, if all the incidents were connected. Hearing him say it out loud brought back her fear that someone could get hurt. But she was pissed that he thought pushing her away was the right way to keep her safe. Getting up, she walked over to stand in front of him, her eyes flashing with the fire he'd ignited. "Don't you think it should be up to me whether to continue to be seen with you or not? Since it's my safety we're debating and not yours? And how do you know this is all about you? Two of the incidents had nothing to do with you. And speaking of, you haven't mentioned if you learned anything by looking up my new donor."

Carter's forehead wrinkled as he gave her a deep scowl. "Keeping people safe is my job, so no, I don't think it should be up to you. Not entirely. You've never seen what it looks like when a situation like this goes south."

If she'd been a cartoon, smoke and flames would have shot out her ears. Cop or not, she was still capable of gauging the risks of their involvement.

"And yes, I have learned some things. Namely, she doesn't exist."

Some of Mara's anger disappeared as she took in that piece of information. "What?"

"I found plenty of Constance Millers, but none with a husband named Kyle who died."

"Why would she lie?"

"I don't know. But I'm going to find out. My gut is

screaming at me that she's connected to everything. I don't have a shred of evidence to suggest that, but that look she gave me in the hallway—" He paused, shaking his head. "If looks could kill, I'd be a dead man."

Mara glanced past him to stare at the street outside, her mind spinning. None of this made any sense. She returned her gaze to him. "Carter—"

He took her hands, cutting her off. "Honey, the last thing I want is to hurt you. This isn't easy for me, either, but if I stick around, you're going to get hurt. And I couldn't live with myself if that happened."

"But what if I do anyway, and you're not here to help?"

His jaw worked. He rubbed her knuckles with his thumbs. "I think it's still a bigger risk for me to stick around. If I leave, the attention goes with me."

"You hope."

Carter let out a long sigh. "Look, we can stand here and debate this or we can try to enjoy the rest of our evening. I don't know about you, but I'd really rather do the latter."

Mara's anger returned. He wanted to pretend like he wasn't putting speed brakes on their relationship with the light of day tomorrow and just go about tonight like nothing was wrong? Oh, hell no.

She turned her frosty blue stare on him. "How about neither? If you're so determined your presence is harmful, why don't you just go?"

Hurt flashed in his eyes; there and gone in a blink. His shoulders straightened and a stoic mask fell over his face, obliterating any trace of what he was thinking or feeling. "That might be best."

"I think so, yes." Her heart shattered as she uttered the words. The hope she had for their future quickly shriveled up and laid down in a corner of her soul.

With a nod and one last, lingering look, he stepped around her. "I'll just get my stuff and we'll be out of your hair."

Mara crossed her arms, turning to watch him walk away. She blinked hard and clenched her teeth, determined to put a mask on her face that matched his. The idiot didn't need to know how much he'd just hurt her.

It only took him a few minutes to gather his things and tote them out to his truck. Once the last load was secured, he came inside to stand near the door. With a sharp whistle, he called Maverick. The dog trotted to his side.

"I'll call you tomorrow. If you need anything—"

"I'll call Brooke or Gemma. Thanks."

His jaw worked, and he nodded. Fleeting hesitation crossed his features a moment before he leaned down and pressed a tender kiss to her cheek. Mara's eyes fluttered shut, and she felt the press of tears. She clenched her teeth to keep them at bay and clenched her fists to stop herself from grabbing his shirt and holding him close.

He raised his head. "I'll see you later." Those liquid silver eyes held her gaze for a long moment, then he abruptly spun on his heel and let himself and Maverick out.

The door clicked shut, and Mara let out the breath she didn't realize she'd been holding. The tears came with it. Flicking the deadbolt closed, she turned and leaned her back against the door, needing the support. Her thoughts rioted, flitting through her mind before she could get more than a feeling from each one. Anger, disbelief, heartbreak. They were all there in some form. One thought was crystal-clear, though. She was glad she never told him she loved him. It would have made this so much worse.

TWENTY-SEVEN

Heavy bass from the speakers flanking the stage reverberated through Mara's chest. She took a sip of her beer and stared at the band playing without seeing them. The country group was pretty good, but she couldn't tell anyone what songs they'd played in the twenty minutes she'd been here. Brooke needed to hurry up. Mara's whole reason for wanting to meet at Big Jimmy's was for the distraction the place provided. They had live music Friday and Saturday nights. But she needed Brooke's larger-than-life personality here to keep her out of her head. The music wasn't enough.

Growling at herself, she took another drink and forced her mind onto the band and off her problems with Carter. She might have been okay if he hadn't called. If it had been a clean break. But he'd failed to get Constance Miller's phone number, so he called to get that Wednesday morning. And he hadn't called since. She'd received two texts, just checking in, but that was all. It left her wanting more. She wanted to hear his voice, not read it on a screen. Better yet, she wanted to have him in front of her so she could touch him and smell him.

"Sorry I'm late." Brooke swooped in and sank into the

chair next to Mara. "Johnathan's being a dumbass." She slapped a hand on the table. "But we're not here to talk about my man problems. We're here to talk about yours. Spill."

Mara blinked at the rapid transition. "Hi. Glad you could come."

Brooke giggled. "Sorry. You know I hate being late. It makes me antsy, then I talk faster."

"You talk fast, anyway." Mara smiled.

"I do. But I'll hush now. You talk." Brooke shrugged out of her coat and looked around for a waitress so she could order a drink.

Letting out a sigh, Mara picked at the label on her beer bottle. "I think Carter and I broke up."

"You don't know?" Brooke's attention returned to Mara. She put her forearms on the table and leaned closer, listening.

"Not really, no. He thinks being around me is putting me in danger. Because of all the stuff that's been happening. He's convinced he's at the center of it and that distancing himself from me will keep me safe."

"So he broke up with you?"

"He said we needed to not see each other until they catch whoever's behind the vandalism attacks. But that we can call and text." She let out a snort. "I've gotten one phone call and two text messages since Wednesday morning." She shook her head. "He didn't leave on the best terms Tuesday night. I was pretty upset and thought he was making a terrible decision. And I was angry that he was making decisions for me. It's my life he's worried about. Shouldn't my opinion matter?"

"Yes, absolutely. But you also can't discount his concerns."

"I know. And I didn't plan to, but he didn't give me a choice in the matter. It was, 'We can't see each other while this is going on, and that's final.' I had no input." Just thinking about it made her angry all over again.

"Men are dumb."

"Agreed." Mara tipped her beer bottle up and took another drink.

"At least his heart was in the right place, though."

"Huh?" Mara lowered the bottle.

"He wouldn't have pushed you away if he didn't care about you."

She'd considered that, but it didn't change the fact that he took the choice away from her. If he wanted back in her good graces, he needed to do some serious groveling. And promise not to do it again. She refused to be in a relationship where she wasn't an equal partner. No matter how much she loved him.

"It still doesn't make it okay."

"No, but I also don't think this is the end for you guys. You need to talk to him."

A grimace scrunched up Mara's face. "I know. I've been waiting until I can do it without losing my temper. So far, I haven't been able to even think about it without getting pissed off again."

Brooke giggled. "Well, how about we see if we can loosen you up a bit?" She stood up and took Mara's beer, setting it on the table before she grabbed her hand and dragged her from her seat. "Maybe if we can get you to relax, you can let some of that anger go."

"Oh, God. What are you doing?"

"Making you dance." Brooke pulled her into the throng of people two-stepping to the beat.

Mara groaned.

"Oh, come on." Brooke laughed and pulled her into line with several other people. "I know you know how to do this."

She did, but it had been a long time since she line-danced. Knowing Brooke would bug her until she caved, Mara gave in. "Fine." Tuning into the music, she let muscle-memory take over and joined in with the crowd.

The rhythm filled her. With each stomp of her boots and

clap of her hands, some of the tension lining her shoulders faded. By the third song, she was a sweaty mess, but smiling freely. When the band switched to a slow number, they went back to their table.

"I'm going to find myself a drink. You want a new beer or a soda?" Brooke pointed to the beer bottle Mara had been nursing before they danced. They both knew better than to drink from an unattended bottle.

"A soda is fine."

"Okay. I'll be right back." Brooke spun away.

Mara swiped at her face and fanned herself. She'd worked up a sweat, dancing in the hot bar. But it had been fun. Her friend was right. It loosened her up. And cleared her mind. She was still angry, but it didn't burn white-hot now.

Brooke returned with their drinks, handing Mara a clear glass filled with dark liquid as she sat down.

"Thanks." Mara pulled what was left of the paper wrapper off the top of the straw and took a big gulp. "Oh, that's good. I'm warm."

"Me too."

"So." Mara gave her friend a side-eyed glance. "Why's Johnathan being a dumbass?"

Brooke rolled her eyes. "He's mad because Grandpa won't let him develop some property along the river. He came home fired up, ranting about how the company was losing millions by leaving it 'pristine'." She air-quoted and rolled her eyes.

Mara shook her head. Lately, she couldn't help but wonder what Brooke saw in Johnathan. He was obsessed with making money. To the point he put Brooke second to it.

"I told him that land was family land. It's the first piece of property my great-great-grandpa ever bought. Where he built a home for his family. Grandpa grew up there. It's not meant for outsiders." She huffed. "Johnathan just doesn't get that.

Drives me nuts. Even more so when he tries to put me in the middle."

"Did he want you to talk to your grandpa?"

Brooke nodded. "I told him no. That led to a shouting match." She paused and glanced away for a moment. "I'm starting to wonder if this marriage is the best idea."

So was Mara. "Men suck."

Brooke raised her glass. "I'll drink to that."

Twenty-Eight

Headlights sweeping the front of her house, Mara pulled into her driveway as a yawn cracked her jaw. She'd stayed out much too late, but she felt better about the situation with Carter after all the dancing and girl-time with Brooke. Things weren't over with him, but they definitely needed to talk.

Pushing the button to open the garage door, she frowned when it stayed closed. Stopping in the drive, Mara pushed the button over the rearview mirror again, but still the door stayed down. She groaned. "Oh, I do not need this now. Why won't you work?" Putting the car in park, she leaned over and dug into the glove compartment for the actual remote. Her fingers closed around the device, and she pushed the button.

Sitting up, she looked at the door. It was still shut. "Great." With a sigh, she shut off the car. "This couldn't have happened yesterday, so I could call a repairman before the weekend?" Shaking her head, she snatched her purse from the passenger seat and got out. Now, she'd have to wait until Monday before she could find anyone to fix it. At least there wasn't any snow in the forecast.

Mara stalked across the driveway and up the path to her front door, searching through her key ring for her house key. With the right one in hand, she put it in the lock and thrust the front door open. As her right foot cleared the threshold, it caught on something, and she stumbled. Her purse and keys hit the floor as she lost her balance.

"What the heck?" She turned, glancing down. A thin, translucent wire fluttered in the breeze. It looked like a piece of fishing line. "Where did that come from?" Bending down, she reached for it, but it was stuck. Her eyes followed it to see where it was hung up. It was tucked behind her welcome sign. She straightened and flipped on the porch light, then grabbed the board and shifted it. What it could be caught on back there, she didn't know. The house, maybe.

Glancing down, Mara's blood froze in her veins, and her lungs stopped working. Her feet worked fine, though. She stumbled back, tripping on the threshold again as she dove into the house and slammed the door. The line was tied to some sort of large grenade.

Heart thundering in her ears, she snagged her purse and ran deeper into the house, one hand in the bag searching for her phone as she went. With several walls between herself and the door, she unlocked her phone. Her fingers found Carter's name in her contacts by rote. She might be angry at his macho-male bullcrap, but there wasn't anyone she would trust more to handle this.

"Mara?" His sleep-roughened voice came over the line. "Wha—"

"There's a grenade outside my front door!" She didn't wait for him to finish.

Half a beat went by. "A grenade?"

"Yes! It was attached to fishing line or something. I tripped over it. When I went to pick up the line, I found it."

"Wait, it didn't go off?"

"No."

"Where are you now?" His voice carried a hard edge. Mara heard him moving around.

"In my bathroom with the door locked."

"You stay there. Don't come out until I or another officer come in and get you."

"Okay. Hurry. And be careful. I didn't check the other doors."

"I will. Stay put." The line clicked.

Mara pulled the phone away from her ear and drew in a shaky breath. She knew he'd hurry, but it would never be fast enough.

TWENTY-NINE

Carter broke every traffic law on the books on his way to Mara's with the aid of his lights and siren. Maverick barked from the back, sensing his handler's worry. The noise drowned out the sound of dispatch calling all units to Mara's house, so he cranked up the volume. He wanted to hear if someone reported anything new. He wasn't the closest unit to her.

"Dammit!" He slammed his hand against the steering wheel. Leaving her alone had been stupid. After the other incidents involving her, he should have known she'd still be a target. But all he'd been able to think about was how the last time people he cared about were in danger, it was he who got them killed. How he hadn't done his job and kept them safe. History was repeating itself. He'd messed up again, and Mara might pay the price. He couldn't let that happen. All that mattered now was that he got to her before something happened. To make sure she was safe.

He swung around the corner into her neighborhood, screeching to a halt at the end of her driveway. Another unit—from the city police—was parked in front of the neighbor's.

The officer had the door open and one foot on the ground, radio in his hand as Carter emerged from his car.

Maverick's barking increased, but Carter left him in the cruiser. Until he knew what they were dealing with, he didn't want the dog stumbling into something that could get him and others killed.

Rounding the hood of his car, he waved at the officer. "I'm going to find a way in."

"What?" The officer popped out of his car, frowning. "We should wait for the bomb squad."

"We should. But I'm not." Ben could suspend him; he didn't care. He wasn't leaving Mara alone in that house a moment longer than necessary.

Carter clicked on his flashlight and jogged toward the structure and down the side of the garage toward the rear. With every step he took, he checked for more triggers and devices. Skills he hadn't used in years came back with ease as he looked for anything that could signal a hidden explosive. Reaching the back door, he scanned the ground, then the doorframe. It looked clear. He lifted a booted foot and kicked in the door.

Wood splintered, and the door flew inward, crashing into the wall, then bouncing back. Carter drew his weapon, keeping it at his side. Mara hadn't said anyone was in the house, but he wasn't about to be caught unaware.

He put up his free hand and pushed the ruined door out of the way, then walked inside. With long, determined strides, he walked through the kitchen. After a quick glance in the living room, he headed down the hallway to the master bedroom.

"Mara?"

The bathroom door flew open. Mara darted out in a blur. Carter caught her against his side, a heap of relief flooding him at the knowledge she was safe.

"Oh, baby. Are you okay?" He pulled back to look into her face. "You're sure you're not hurt anywhere?"

"I'm fine. Just scared. Get me out of here."

Carter nodded. He could feel the fine tremor running through her body. "The back door was clear. Let's go back that way." He took her hand and retraced his steps. In moments, they were jogging around the side of the house and out front, where the police presence had increased. Two county cruisers and another local unit now flanked his car and blocked the street. Neighbors also stood on their lawns, watching the commotion.

He eyed the throng of people, spotting Ben. Letting out a sharp whistle, Carter headed that way.

"Townsend, I ought to suspend your ass." Ben crossed his arms and glared.

"Go for it. I wasn't leaving her in there." Carter held Ben's stare. He wasn't sorry.

Jaw working for a long moment as he stared at Carter, Ben finally dropped his arms, his expression clearing. "Don't do it again." He turned his attention to Mara. "Are you all right?"

"I'm fine."

"What happened?"

Carter looked at her, wanting to hear more of the story himself.

"I went out with Brooke tonight. To Big Jimmy's. We had a beer, about three glasses of soda, and danced for a few hours. When I got home, my garage door wouldn't open, so I went through the front door."

"What was wrong with the garage door?" Carter's gaze strayed to the garage.

"I don't know. Neither the button on my mirror nor the remote that came with the house would work. I figured there was something wrong with the motor."

"Okay," Ben said. "What happened next?"

"As I walked over the threshold, my foot caught on something, and I tripped. When I glanced back, there was a piece of what looked like fishing line fluttering. I thought something had blown onto my porch and I just got my feet caught in it. But when I reached down to pick up the line to throw it away, it was caught on something behind the welcome sign." She pointed at the board leaning against the house on the porch.

Carter sucked in a breath. "You pulled on it?" Dear God, but she was lucky to be alive.

She nodded. "Not hard. It's fishing line; I figured it would slide free. When it didn't, I turned on the light and moved the sign, and that's when I saw the canister."

"What color was it?" Carter asked.

"Green."

"How big?"

She let go of his hand to hold her hands up about a foot apart, then curved her fingers to make a six-inch circle.

"You're sure it was that big?"

"Yes. I was eye-level with it. It wasn't small. Why?"

Carter caught Ben's eye. "Because that's too large for a grenade."

A slight widening of Ben's eyes was his only tell before he backed up, spinning away. "We need to widen the perimeter." He jogged the few steps to his car and ducked his head inside.

"Carter, what's going on? Why is he so worried all of a sudden?"

He pushed her toward his car and his barking dog. "Because I think that's a land mine on your front porch."

"What? Geez! What the hell is going on?"

"I don't know, but I'm going to find out." He opened the passenger door. The sound of Maverick's barks increased. Carter ignored him and pushed Mara inside. The car wouldn't stop all the shrapnel should the mine explode, but it would catch the brunt of it. "Stay low." Once she had her feet tucked in, he ran around to the driver's side and got in, starting the engine.

"Where are we going?"

"Down the block, out of the blast radius." He backed up and turned around, driving down the street and parked across the road. "What else can you tell me about the device? Did it have smooth sides? What about spikes coming off the top?"

"It looked like a large can with a tube coming off the top and three prongs sticking up from the top of that. And yes, the sides were smooth."

Carter's heartbeat quickened. Definitely not a grenade. "Okay. Anything else? Writing?"

She glanced to the side briefly, then nodded. "It was yellow. And it looked like German."

Unease rippled through him. If that was the type of mine he thought it was, it could be extremely unstable. Leaving the engine running, he opened the door. "Stay inside." He reached between the seats and opened the kennel door so she had access to Mav. "If you need me, flip this switch." He pointed to a panel above her head. "Just flick it back and forth. It'll sound the siren."

"Carter—"

He laid a finger over her lips. "Please, Mara. I need to go help evacuate your neighbors, but I also need to know you're safe."

She rolled her lips in, pressing them together. "Okay. Please be careful."

"I will." Leaning over the console, he kissed her. "Blast the siren if you need help." Sliding out of the car, he shut the door and jogged away.

Running up the road, he dodged the other officers who were moving their vehicles back and headed for the closest house to the blast zone. It was the elderly couple who lived next door. If the mine exploded, shrapnel would go through the window on the side of their house and into the living room. At this hour, it wouldn't normally be an issue, but the activity had roused them from their bed. He could see the living room lights on.

House by house, he and the other officers went until the neighbors were all down the block, past the perimeter they'd established.

"That everyone?" Ben asked, jogging up.

"I think so."

"Good. Bomb squad is on the way, but it'll be another forty-five minutes." He shook his head. "Once things settle down, I think I need to find a way to get some basic EOD stuff for the sheriff's department. This is happening much too frequently for my liking."

Carter gave a short nod. "I agree. I wish we had the equipment too. I'd already be up there looking at that thing." Instead, he was forced to stand here and wait for Asheville's bomb squad. But the moment they arrived, he'd be asking for a suit to go with them.

While they waited, Carter split his time between jogging to the car to check on Mara and talking to the neighbors to see if anyone saw or heard anything. He came up with zeros. There were enough shadows on Mara's porch in that corner no one noticed anyone. By the time the bomb squad arrived, he was ready for some answers.

Ben hurried over, joining Carter as he approached their vehicle.

"Sheriff." The commander of the unit, Matt Gunderson, stepped out of the driver's side. "Fill me in."

Ben gave him a quick rundown.

"You're sure it's a land mine?" His gaze wandered between Ben and Carter.

"We haven't laid eyes on it, but based on Mara's description, that would be my guess. I think it's a World War II-era

German S-mine. What most people know as a Bouncing Betty."

Gunderson frowned. "Where would someone get one of those?"

"Black market." Carter crossed his arms. "But they're lucky it didn't go off before they ever got it here. After almost eighty years, those things are highly unstable."

"That's no lie." Gunderson cocked his head. "You former EOD?"

Carter nodded. "I had a detection dog. I was going to ask to suit up with whoever you send in. I've seen Betty's before. Not many, but insurgents did use them."

"That's fine by me. Sheriff?"

Ben nodded. "If you're willing."

"Sure. None of my guys have ever seen one outside of the classroom. Myself included." He tipped his head toward the rear of the truck. "Come on. Let's get you suited up."

Carter followed the man around to the double doors and climbed in behind him. After some quick introductions, Gunderson's men helped the two of them into bomb suits.

Nerves blasted Carter. He wrapped a hand around the neckline of the suit and tugged, trying to make some room. But it wasn't the tightness of the outfit that truly bothered him. He hadn't been around explosives—except in training— since he left the Marines. That part of his mind where his guilt over what happened to his squadmates lived rebelled at the idea of going in to defuse another explosive.

He dropped his hand and clenched his fists. This wasn't the time or place for him to relive the past. It didn't help him now. It wouldn't ever. No, right now, he needed to stay in the present and do his best to get the device under control and make it safe, so no one got hurt.

"You ready?" Gunderson picked up a tool kit. The others

were going to have the robot bring a lead-lined box up the drive and wait.

Carter nodded and reached for his helmet, putting it on. Gunderson did the same, then tested their communications. His voice rang into Carter's ears loud and clear.

"How do you want to approach this?" Gunderson asked as they headed toward the house.

"Slowly. With its age, vibrations could set it off if it's rusted enough."

"That woman's lucky. It's a miracle she didn't set it off."

That same knife that twisted his gut when Mara called to tell him about the device dug deeper. Gunderson didn't need to tell him how lucky she was to be alive. He was fully aware.

When they reached the porch, they took slow, steady steps, rolling their feet to avoid jarring the floorboards. Once they were close enough, Carter took a breath to steel his nerves and grabbed the welcome sign, moving it to the side.

Gunderson let out a low whistle. "Yeah, that ain't no grenade."

"Definitely not. Have them roll the robot and box closer. We're going to have to pick this thing up. Unless your robot can climb stairs?"

"Nope. I keep asking for that kind, but I keep getting denied. So we just pick Herbie up and carry him. It's never been a problem until now when the device is vibration sensitive."

"Well, use this the next time you ask. Maybe they'll give you a longer arm too."

"That'd be nice."

"It would," Carter said, distracted as he played out his path to the robot. "Have your men roll the robot there." He pointed to a spot at the edge of the porch. "I don't want to go any further than necessary."

Relaying the information, Gunderson swiveled to watch

the robot roll closer. Carter crouched, shining his light on the device to get a better look. It was in fairly good shape. Less rust than on some he'd seen. This one had probably been stored well somewhere. He could see the fishing line still attached to the safety pin. It wasn't in all the way, but it was in far enough to have kept the mine from exploding. Whoever set it up did a poor job. The tripwire wasn't supposed to give on the anchor end.

"How's that?"

Carter glanced back. Gunderson pointed to the robot. It was in position and had the box elevated so he wouldn't have to bend to put the mine inside. "Works. Get the lid off the box."

"You sure you don't want me to pick that up?"

"I'm sure." This wasn't the first mine he'd handled. He knew what he was doing. Wrapping his gloved hands around the canister, he rose and pivoted in one smooth movement. In three rolling strides, he crossed the porch and set the device inside the box.

Gunderson moved in with the lid.

"Careful." Carter held up a hand. "Set it down slow. That pin was hanging. If it goes off before we lock it, it'll blow the lid off."

"Not my first rodeo." Gunderson laid the lid on top.

Carter helped him secure the latches, then Gunderson radioed for his men to back the robot away from the house. Holding his breath, Carter watched it roll over the grass, then down the driveway to the middle of the road. It lowered the box, then backed away. The two men walked to the truck and around to the rear.

Gunderson pulled off his helmet and addressed one of his men. "Give me the disposal charge and roll that robot back here."

The robot appeared around the door. Carter stepped back

so Gunderson's crew could change out the arm on the machine. They were going to remotely detonate the charge and set off the mine in the box.

Once the robot was ready, Carter watched on the screen built into the wall of the truck as Gunderson piloted the robot up to the box and unlatched it. After checking the scene was secure, he armed the disposal charge and dropped it inside, then latched the box once more. A minute later, a soft boom shook the quiet night. The lead box rocked. Carter breathed a sigh of relief that the mine was no longer a threat.

THIRTY

A loud bark in her ear snapped Mara's eyes open. Heart thundering in her chest, she glanced back at Maverick. He whined and licked her face.

"Oh!" She wiped her cheek. "Thanks, Mav."

Tapping on her window made her jump, and she let out a soft shriek. Maverick barked again, his front feet on the console as he leaned around her, barking at the dark-haired man on the other side of the window.

"Hush." Where was Carter? She wasn't about to open the door. She wouldn't put it past the dog to climb over her and rush out. Instead, she cracked the window. "Yes?"

"Ma'am, I'm Agent Finley Porter, ATF." He held up a badge. "Can you answer a few questions for me?"

"Sure." She had to yell to be heard over the dog. "Could you find Carter first? I don't want to open this door." She gestured to the furious animal at her side.

He nodded and turned away.

Mara glanced at Maverick. "You're a menace. He's going to have to teach me to handle you."

His barks changed to yips and whines. She reached up and

scratched his neck with a sigh, which quickly morphed into a yawn. It was late. Almost morning, really. At least it was Saturday, so she didn't have to go to work. Once she finished answering the multitude of questions sure to come her way and the cops cleared her house—and someone sealed up her back door—she planned to crawl into her bed and sleep. The catnap she just had wasn't nearly enough.

Through the windshield, she saw Carter and Agent Porter walking over. Ben was with them, as was another man she didn't recognize. Carter came around to the driver's side and opened the rear door. Maverick disappeared into his kennel in a flurry of whines and toenail scrabbles. He was ready to get out. Mara knew how he felt. She was tired of being cooped up too.

Rolling her window down, she poked her head out and looked at Ben. "Can I get out?"

He nodded.

Thank Heavens. She opened the door and swung her legs out, wincing as she stood up. Her back and hips ached from being stuck in the car so long.

"Mara, Agent Porter said he introduced himself." Ben stopped in front of her and gestured to the tall, dark-haired man at his side.

"He did."

Ben's head bobbed once, then he pointed to the other man with them. "This is the local police chief, Randy Cage."

The older man nodded to her. "Ma'am."

Mara offered him a tired smile.

"Mrs. Roth, I just need to ask you some questions about what happened. I know you already talked to Deputy Townsend, and he's relayed what you said, but I'd like to hear it from you, if you don't mind?" Agent Porter tipped his head to Carter, who came up beside Mara.

"Of course."

"Great. Can you start at the beginning? Walk me through what happened."

Mara took a breath and started her tale, recounting what she'd told Carter.

"You didn't notice anyone or anything out of the ordinary when you pulled in?" Agent Porter asked. "Maybe a car that doesn't belong in the neighborhood? Or a shadow that didn't look like one you've seen a million times?"

"There were a lot of shadows I haven't seen before. I'm not normally out so late. But no, I didn't see anything that made me look twice. Everything looked like it always does."

"What about inside?" Ben asked. "Was anything different in the house? The bomb squad checked for explosives and didn't find anything other than the one on the porch, but they couldn't tell if anything was missing or out of place. The only other issue they found was that someone cut the power to your garage. Likely so you'd go through the front door."

She swallowed hard. Tonight shouldn't have ended so well for her. "Honestly, I didn't look. I saw the mine, freaked out and ran. I locked myself in my bathroom and called Carter." She gestured to the man standing beside her. "When he arrived, we didn't linger. He led me out through the back door and put me in his cruiser. I've been there since."

"Okay." Porter glanced at the others. "Sheriff Davidson said y'all have been having some trouble around here with vandalism. And possibly a fraud scheme?"

Mara nodded, but it was Carter who spoke.

"All of it has centered around the two of us. Me more than her. I think whatever it is has to do with me, and she's been caught in the crossfire."

"Tell me about these incidents." Porter shifted his stance and put his hands in his pockets, attention firmly focused on them.

Carter related everything that led up to this point. Mara

chimed in with a few details and with her account of her meeting with Constance Miller.

"She's your only suspect?" Porter glanced at Ben, who nodded.

"Viable one, yes. Carter's pulled a few from cases he's worked in the past. My detectives are looking into them, but no one's really stood out yet except for her."

"Have you learned any more about her?"

Ben shook his head. "She gave a false name, and the phone number she called Mara on is a burner. We haven't been able to trace it."

Porter looked at Carter. "This isn't some crazy ex, is it?"

"No. I met her in the hallway at the equestrian center as she was leaving Tuesday. I don't know her."

"You're sure?"

"Hundred percent. But she seemed to know me. Glared daggers as she passed by."

"You have surveillance cameras at the center, yes?" Porter asked Mara.

"Yes."

"I need the footage. I'll get a warrant to run facial recognition on her. Maybe we'll get lucky."

A sliver of hope lit in Mara's chest. She prayed the agent got something from the cameras. They needed to figure out what was going on before she or Carter were seriously injured. Or worse.

THIRTY-ONE

Cool wind whipped past Mara's face as she darted through the outdoor arena astride Stinger. Despite the chill, it promised to be a beautiful day, for which she was glad. Yesterday had been one of the longest days of her life, and she needed the relaxation riding provided. She had half a mind to load her horse into the trailer and head into the wilderness for a trail ride. Only the knowledge that someone tried to kill her and going off alone was dumb kept her riding around barrels in the arena. It probably wasn't wise for her to be here by herself, either, but she couldn't stay in her house alone anymore.

When they parted ways early Saturday morning after he fixed the gaping hole where her back door used to be, Carter promised to stop by later. He never did. She received a text telling her he got hung up with an emergency and that he'd try to catch her Sunday. Mara had no doubt he'd been at work. It just irked her that he couldn't even call. Or swing by, even for a couple minutes, to tell her.

She leaned into the final turn and gave Stinger his head. The horse sailed through the dirt to the end of the arena. Mara sat up and pulled on the reins. A sharp bark made her look to her left. Carter stood along the fence with Maverick. Her silly heart skipped a beat.

Nudging Stinger's sides, she trotted over. "Hey."

"Hey."

"How did you find me?" She was betting Ben told him. He was the only one who knew where she was. She'd called Gemma on her way out the door and asked her to tell Ben where she was headed. Just in case.

Carter shrugged. "You weren't home. I figured you were here or went to the store. I came here first."

Stinger shifted, not done with his workout. She reined him in, and he tossed his head, not happy to be standing still. "What's up?"

"We need to talk."

"Agreed, but you're either going to have to ride with me or wait." Stinger shifted again.

"I'll wait. I don't think he'll be content with the pace you'd have to keep with me." He nodded to her horse.

No, he most definitely would not. "Okay. I shouldn't be too much longer. We've been out here about twenty minutes already."

"Take your time. I'm not going anywhere."

The look in his eyes told Mara his words held a deeper meaning. A little of her ire diminished. The part that stemmed from the fear he didn't want to be with her.

She gave him a quick nod and spun Stinger around, taking off along the fence line.

Thirty-Two

Carter leaned on the fence rail and watched Mara ride around the arena on the black streak she called a horse. Her red ponytail streamed behind her like a flag and dirt flew from the horse's hooves as he rounded barrels and charged forward. How she stayed on, Carter didn't know. There were times she leaned so far her knees nearly skimmed the dirt. But she always kept her seat, moving with the horse as he ran.

She had him captivated. Not just with her skill, but with her ferocity. It was a practice session, but rider and horse attacked the course like they were riding for gold. Mara did everything with her whole heart.

Knowing that, is what kept him away yesterday. Why he texted instead of called. He'd needed time to think. Once the dust settled, and his adrenaline ebbed, the knowledge of what could have been punched him in the gut. He'd muddled through debriefings on his part in securing the mine, then drove home and stumbled into bed. There, he'd laid awake, his thoughts running a hundred miles an hour as he processed his feelings.

And his memories. Once he let in thoughts about what

happened all those years ago, the floodgates opened, and he couldn't stop the tide of emotion. For the first time since the explosion, he'd let himself cry. Not just a tear or two, but a whole bucket full of tears. It was a true catharsis that washed away a lot of the guilt he still held. He'd always wonder if maybe it was his fault, but he was done blaming himself. There were too many what-ifs for anyone to ever know for sure what happened.

When he'd calmed, he'd debated for a hot minute going to Mara's house and crawling into bed with her, but he knew they needed to talk before that could happen. Not wanting to wake her after the night she had, he went home with every intention of going by later. But a lost hiker changed his plans, and he and Maverick set off into the woods to help with the search.

He should have called. Texting was the coward's way of bowing out of his promise to come see her. Which was why he was here now. Calling wouldn't have smoothed things over. It might have made things worse. He'd made plenty of mistakes in the last few days. He didn't need to make more. She was angry enough. Carter could see it in every line of her body whenever she glanced at him.

That was okay. She had every right to be upset with him. He'd been a dumbass and was ready to admit that. He just hoped it was enough.

Mara slowed her horse to a trot, making circles around the arena. After several passes, she slowed to a walk. After her second pass, she called out to him.

"Meet me at the gate."

Carter pushed away from the fence and followed along it to the gate. He swung it open, and she walked through, still on her horse. The animal's hooves clip-clopped on the concrete floor as she rode him to his stall.

Inside the stables, Maverick roamed from stall to stall,

sniffing each one. Carter kept one eye on him and stopped beside Mara. She swung off her horse in one smooth movement, her boots making a soft thud as she landed.

"Do you want help?"

She shook her head and reached for the strap going around the horse's stomach. Loosening it, she pulled on the saddle, and it slid off the animal's back.

Carter stepped forward and took it from her. "Where does it go?"

"Tack room. Down the hall." She pointed deeper into the barn.

He remembered seeing it when he was here before. Striding away, he put her saddle where it belonged. When he walked back, she had a large comb in her hand and was busy brushing the horse. Not knowing what else to do, he leaned against the wall and watched.

"You're really good with him."

She shrugged. "I've been riding all my life."

"What's his name?" He nodded to the horse.

"Stinger."

Carter smiled. "That fits. He attacked that course. Do you use him for therapy sessions too?"

"Yes. He's good with the older riders. I wouldn't put a child on him. But our military guys love him." She cast a glance at him. "But you didn't come here to talk about my horse."

No, he didn't. Taking a deep breath, he dove in head first. "I'm sorry. You were right, and I should have listened to you."

Her movements slowed, then picked up again, and she stayed silent.

"I let my fears override my brain, and the very thing I was trying to avoid came true."

She stopped and turned to look at him. "If something hadn't happened, would you have come back?"

"I always intended to. Stepping back from your life was only temporary."

Mara waved the comb at him. "See, that's the problem. You thought you could dictate how our relationship would work. That's why I'm upset still. I'm not interested in being lorded over, Carter. This is either an equal partnership or we aren't a thing. You can't make unilateral decisions that affect both of us."

He'd come to that realization himself when she gave him one and two-word answers when he called the other day. But he'd convinced himself staying away was best for her. In reality, he'd just been scared by the feelings she made him feel.

Carter walked forward and took her hands, comb and all. "I know I was wrong, and I'm sorry. I truly do want what's best for you, but I promise never to make that kind of decision on my own again. We'll always discuss it first. I want us to be a team. You mean a lot to me, Mara. I don't want to lose you. Not to some crazed idiot out for revenge, and certainly not to my own stupidity."

A soft smile crossed her face. "I'll make sure to call you out on your stupidity. So long as you listen to me, we should be fine."

"Oh, really?" A low chuckle emanated from his chest. He tugged her into his body and wrapped his arms around her. Sobering, he stared down at her. "I truly am sorry, Mara. Can we start over?"

Bright blue eyes studied him for a long moment before she nodded. "Yeah. I think that would be great."

A wide smile split his face, and he leaned down. "Good." He closed the distance between them and kissed her. Fireworks exploded behind his eyes. He'd missed this. Missed her. He had no intention of ever letting her go again.

THIRTY-THREE

The ring of Mara's phone startled her out of the sea of numbers swimming before her eyes. This was the part of her job she hated. Quarterlies. Eyes still on the screen, she lifted the receiver and tucked it into her shoulder. "Mara Roth."

"Mara, I'm so glad I caught you. The police called and said there was a problem with the check I wrote you?"

Sitting up straight, Mara blinked as her brain switched gears. "Ms. Miller?"

"Yes. Sorry, I forgot to say that, didn't I? I'm just so upset about this check. They wouldn't tell me what was wrong. Just that there was a problem, and they needed to speak with me. Can you give me any more information?"

Oh, boy. When she turned that check over to Carter, she hadn't anticipated Constance Miller calling about it again.

"Well, I'm not too sure what's going on." That was the God's honest truth. "My accountant requested more information before we cashed it. He must have contacted the police for some reason." That was not the God's honest truth. "You'll have to do as the police asked, I'm afraid." She bit back a snort.

They hadn't asked her to do squat. They couldn't reach her if they couldn't find her. Mara didn't know what game Constance was playing at, but Mara could play too. And by her own set of rules.

"Are you sure? I was hoping to clear this up with a quick meeting. Would you be able to meet me for lunch today?"

Alarm bells went off in Mara's brain. After everything that had happened and the suspicions surrounding this woman and her money, Mara wasn't meeting her anywhere. Not alone, anyway. "I'm sorry, I'm afraid I'm swamped today. The rest of this week, really. I'm not sure what else I could tell you face-to-face, anyway. I don't really know any more than you do."

Constance sighed. "All right. I guess I'll give that detective a call. Thank you."

"You're welcome. Have a good day."

"You too." She hung up.

Mara stared at the receiver as she put it back in the cradle. That was weird. The woman was definitely fishing for information. Hesitating only a moment, she lifted the phone again and called Carter. His cell rang several times before he answered, winded.

"Hey, hon. What's up? Everything okay?"

"I'm not sure. Are you all right?"

"I'm fine. Maverick and I went for a run. The vet cleared him for active duty, so I'm out making sure he's ready."

"Oh. Is he?"

"He's doing great. But you didn't call to talk about Mav. What's up?"

Mara heaved a sigh and leaned an elbow on her desk, rubbing her forehead. She could feel a headache brewing behind her eyes. "Constance Miller called. She said the police called, wanting to ask her questions about the check she wrote. She asked if I knew anything about that and then asked if I could meet her for lunch today."

"What did you say?"

She could hear in his voice that he didn't like that idea. "That I was too busy, and she should call the police back and ask her questions of them."

"Good."

"Have you learned anything else about her?"

"The number she gave you came back to a burner phone. We still haven't located her car. The number she called you on today, can you read it to me?"

"Oh. Sure." She pushed some buttons on her phone, scrolling to her call history. Finding the previous number, she read it to him. "That's different than the last one."

"It is. I'm going to get this to Ben. Maybe she screwed up, and we'll be able to find her. You okay there at the center?"

"Of course. I'm not going anywhere. I've got numbers to crunch and reports to compile."

"All right. I'll be by later when it's time for you to go home."

"Sounds good. Be careful."

"I will."

The phone clicked in her ear as he hung up. Mara set the handset down. Worried, she stared at the wall. She hoped that new phone number yielded some answers. Before something else happened.

Blowing out a breath, she turned back to her computer. The numbers wouldn't crunch themselves. And she'd like to get a ride in before Carter arrived later to take her home. She could use time to herself to unwind and destress.

Buried in her work, she came up for air long enough to eat the sandwich and fruit she packed, but otherwise stayed locked away until Pam poked her head in.

"Hey, girl. I'm going home. Everybody else already left."

"Oh." Mara looked at the clock in the corner of her screen. It was after five o'clock. "How did it get that late?"

"Time flies when you're having fun."

Chuckling, Mara saved her work and exited out of her programs. "More like time flies when you want to get stuff done so you don't have to worry about it again for three months."

Pam grinned. "That too. Do you want me to wait so I can walk out with you?" Her staff was aware of what was going on.

"Is Carter here?"

"Not yet. Unless he's waiting in the parking lot."

"He'd come in. Or call to tell me he was here. Thanks for the offer, but I'll wait for him to arrive."

"Okay. Well, I'll see you in the morning, then. Have a good night." She waggled her fingers and stepped back into the hall.

Mara smiled. "You too."

Pam closed the door. Mara shut down her computer and gathered her things, piling them on her desk so she could just grab them later. She'd go get that ride in while she waited on Carter—hopefully. Maybe she'd make him wait even if he did arrive soon. She really wanted to ride. It cleared her mind and helped her relax. After today, she could certainly use that. Once she had her stuff gathered up, she exchanged her flats for her riding boots, then left her office. Locking the door behind her, she wandered down the hall and out the door to the arena. Her boots made little noise on the concrete as she walked along the walkway to the stables. Soft whickers greeted her as she turned into the row of stalls. She pet the noses that came over their doors to say hello as she passed.

At Stinger's stall, she opened the door, grabbing the lead rope hanging on the hook on the outer wall. Her horse tossed his head, letting out a quiet whinny as he walked toward her.

"Hey, bud." She rubbed a hand down the middle of his face and snapped the rope onto his halter. "Fancy a ride?"

He leaned into her touch. Mara scratched his head and ears, then backed toward the door. "Come on." She led him out and down the corridor to the tack room. Tying him to the peg on the wall, she went in and retrieved his saddle, blanket, and bridle. With practiced hands, she saddled her horse, then swung onto his back. His hooves clomped on the concrete as she turned him and rode toward the indoor arena. She'd left her coat in her office, plus the outdoor lights weren't on, and they'd take a while to warm up. He'd have to be content doing laps inside tonight.

Out in the soft dirt, she kicked him into a slow trot to warm up his muscles. They did a couple of laps before she nudged him faster, increasing the tempo each time she passed the stables until they moved at a quick canter.

Mara felt some of the stress of her day melt away with each thud of Stinger's hooves in the dirt. This was her happy place. Being with Carter was wonderful, but there was something about being alone on a horse that spoke to her inner self. It set part of her soul free so it could soar without a care in the world.

The bang of a door brought her back down to earth. She slowed Stinger and looked toward the sound, expecting to see Carter. He now had keys to every building she did, so he could come and go as he pleased. They'd done a lot of talking over the last couple of days since their heart-to-heart here the other morning. Mara made it clear she cared about him and wanted to involve him in all aspects of her life. He'd felt the same, so they exchanged keys. He'd also given her her first lesson with Maverick. It went well, but she definitely needed to practice the commands more. Getting the pronunciation down would be key. So would remembering them all. He'd given her a book and a list of websites to help her. She'd been studying and was hopeful she'd do well when they practiced again.

But it wasn't Carter standing at the fence rail. It was Constance Miller.

Mara changed course, a fierce frown on her face as she rode over. "How did you get in here?" Pam would have locked the front doors on her way out. The rear doors were never unlocked anymore. Not after all the trouble they'd had.

"We really need to talk." Constance headed for the gate, a concerned frown on her face. "Get off that horse and come over here."

"What? No. You need to leave. I still want to know how you got in."

Constance's look turned cold. She pulled a matte black handgun from her coat pocket. "I said, get off the horse, Mara."

Mara's blood turned to ice. "Why do you have a gun? What's going on?"

"Get off the horse. I'm not asking again." She raised the weapon, pointing it at Stinger. "Get off or I'll make you get off."

"Hey, whoa. Leave my horse out of this." Mara raised her hands, then grasped the pommel with one hand, rising up to swing her leg over and drop to the ground. "There, I'm down."

"Leave him there. You're coming with me."

Mara thought frantically. She couldn't leave with Constance. That was what all the dumb women in the horror films did. And they ended up dead. She had no intention of leaving this world yet.

She yelped as a shot rang out, and dirt flew at her horse's feet. Stinger reared, his loud whinny echoing off the metal rafters. Mara fought to hold on to him. After several tense seconds, he stopped trying to pull away, but continued to paw at the dirt.

"I won't miss with the next one. If you don't want a dead horse, drop the reins."

Mara let go of the leather straps and walked toward the insane woman. She didn't want to go with her, but she didn't want her horse to die, either. "What's going on? Why are you doing this?"

"It's nothing personal. Not with you, at least. Your boyfriend, though—he's another story."

"Carter? What issue do you have with him?"

Ice flowed from the woman's steel-blue eyes. "He killed my husband."

Thirty-Four

Carter swiped his palm on his pant leg, then rapped his knuckles on the doorframe of Ben's office. His boss glanced up. "Got a minute?" Carter stepped just over the threshold.

"Sure. What's up?"

"Mara got another call from Constance Miller." He held up the piece of paper in his hand. "From a different number."

Ben motioned him forward and took the note. "Have you called this yet?"

"No. I don't want a lawyer to come back and say I interfered in any way." If this woman was behind all their problems, he didn't want her to walk because he couldn't let someone else handle it.

"Good." He lifted his phone, but Carter was surprised to hear him call Tristan and not the number on the note.

Hanging up, Ben glanced at Carter. "Tristan and Jake are handling the case on our end. They're cooperating with ATF now."

Carter bit back a groan. He had nothing against the ATF.

They had better resources. But it meant he couldn't stay in the loop like he could here.

Boots on the tile floor heralded their arrival. Carter stepped to the side to make room.

Ben held up the note. "Find this woman. And let Agent Porter know whatever you find."

"You got it." Nodding to Ben and Carter, Tristan spun around, Jake on his heels, and they left.

"Have you finished those reports?" Ben asked.

Carter sighed. "No." Since he was basically sidelined until Maverick could go back on patrol, Ben had Carter working on a backlog of reports. It was annoying and tedious, but it kept Carter in the thick of things. Hopefully, he could still glean some information, even if things were getting routed through the feds.

"Better get to working, then. They won't catalogue themselves."

Biting back a groan, Carter nodded and left the office. Back at his desk, he settled into his chair and logged into his computer.

The next several hours passed in a slow blur. He did his best to stay focused, so he wouldn't think about things he couldn't do anything about. By late afternoon, he'd made a decent dent in the backlog.

Commotion drew Carter's attention away from his computer screen. He glanced up to see Tristan and Jake putting their coats on and gathering their gear. Rising, Carter took two steps into the aisle, blocking their path. "What did you find?"

Tristan frowned. "How do you know it's about your case?"

Carter crossed his arms. "Is it?"

"Yes."

Nervous excitement erupted in Carter's veins. "And?"

"We got the warrant to execute a search at a motel between here and Asheville. The number is registered to them."

"I'm coming with you." He reached for the leash on his desk.

"Carter—"

Carter held up a hand. "I'll stay out of the way and only get involved if Maverick's needed. We're the only K-9 unit in the county. You might need us."

Tristan eyed him, then the dog, who'd risen to sit next to Carter's desk.

"Has he been cleared for duty?"

"Sort of." Technically, he was cleared, but with the training lapse, Carter hadn't intended to take the dog into the field for another day or two.

Rolling his eyes, Tristan reached for the desk phone. He punched some numbers in and lifted the receiver to his ear.

"Hey, Ben. Can I take Carter and Maverick to execute my search warrant?"

Carter strained to hear what Ben said, but the man's voice was too low for him to make anything out.

"Okay. Sounds good." He hung up. "He said it's up to you. If you think Maverick's well enough to do his job, then yes, you can come."

"He'll be fine. We were going back on duty tomorrow or the next day, anyway."

"Then let's go."

Snagging the rest of his things, including Maverick's harness, he followed Tristan and Jake out of the building.

"Where are we going?" he called as he opened the rear door on his cruiser. Maverick jumped inside.

Jake told him the name of the motel. Carter nodded. He knew where that was. After putting Mav's harness on him, he got in the vehicle. Pulling out behind Tristan and Jake, he followed them to the location, along with another patrol car.

He tapped his fingers on the steering wheel as he drove. It would kill him to stay put while the others executed the warrant, but he meant what he told Ben. He didn't want to jeopardize this case. The only reason he would get involved was if they needed the dog.

They turned into the motel. Carter pulled off to the side and waited while Tristan and Jake went into the main office to talk to the manager. He surveyed the structure in front of him, noting the two-story design and stairwells on both ends. His location gave him the perfect vantage point to watch for anyone trying to sneak away.

A few minutes after they entered, Tristan and Jake came out of the office and Tristan jogged his way. Carter rolled down his window.

"I described Ms. Miller to the manager, and he checked his records. She's staying in room one thirty-one. He doesn't think she's here right now, though. Said she's been driving a black Ford SUV."

"Not a white one?"

Tristan shook his head. "She was, but then showed up with this car last week. The manager said she told him they were both rentals, and the other car had an issue, so she got a new one."

Carter scoffed. "Yeah. It got caught on a security camera. Okay."

"We're going to search her room. Keep an eye out and radio us if you see her."

"Will do."

Tristan backed away, and Carter rolled up the window. Maverick barked, protesting being left behind.

"I know, bud. I want to go with them too."

Through the windshield, he watched the others execute the warrant on Ms. Miller's room. He shifted his car to give him a better view of the road, then kept one eye on the building and the other on cars driving by, hoping to catch her returning. But by the time they finished their search, she was still MIA.

Carter got out of his car, needing to stretch his legs, and jogged over to Tristan and Jake's vehicle, where Jake sat in the driver's seat, writing. "Anything?"

"Maybe." Jake took his phone from his pocket and pulled up some pictures. "She's obsessed with you."

Eyes widening as he took in the folder full of pictures of him, Carter's heartbeat quickened. Who was this woman and why was she so interested in him? "Did you find anything to indicate why she's obsessed with me?"

"No," Jake said. "Just that. We lifted some prints, though. Hopefully, they'll tell us who she really is. You're sure you don't know her?"

"Positive."

"Okay. Well, we're about finished here. I think Tristan might have the uniform stay behind for a little while in case she shows up."

"Sounds good." Carter glanced at the clock on the dash. "I need to get going. I'm already late picking Mara up from work." He was actually surprised she hadn't called. A curl of unease unfurled in his gut.

Jake nodded. "We'll call you if anything shakes out."

"That works." Carter walked away, barely noticing the other man's wave. He was too distracted by the fact Mara hadn't called. Climbing into his cruiser again, he pushed the button on his steering wheel to enable the voice feature that connected his phone to the car. "Call Mara."

The phone rang through the interior. When it rolled to voicemail, he pushed the button to disconnect the call, tapping his fingers against the steering wheel. Pushing the voice button again, he tried her office phone and got the same result. Something wasn't right.

He leaned his head out the window and gave a sharp whistle. Jake poked his head from the car and Tristan stepped back from the rear of it, where he was stowing the evidence they gathered.

"I can't get Mara on the phone."

"You try her cell and the center's number?" Tristan called.

"Yes."

Stepping back, Tristan shut the hatch. "We'll follow you."

With a nod, Carter rolled the window up and put the car in gear. He wasn't waiting on them. They knew the way.

Out on the road, Carter tried Mara's cell again. It went to voicemail once more. So did her office number. Growling, he disconnected the call. Where was she? He supposed it was possible she was riding her horse and didn't have her phone on her. If that was the case, she'd get an earful about not carrying it.

Carter made the fifteen-minute drive back to Foggy Mountain, on edge the entire way. Pulling into the lot, he parked near the door and got out. Maverick barked, not wanting to be left behind. "I hear you, bud." He opened the rear door and clipped the leash to the dog's harness. "Let's go." Maverick hopped down, and Carter headed for the door.

Using the key Mara gave him, he let them into the building. It was quiet. "Mara?" Wandering down the hall, he stopped at her office. The door was closed and locked, the lights off inside. Continuing down the hallway, he went through the door to the arena.

The black horse trotting around the enclosure drew his attention. Alarm bells went off in his head as he noted the saddle on the horse's back. Carter glanced around. "Mara?" Worried now, he jogged down the concourse toward the stables. Had she fallen off her horse and managed to make it to the restroom, only to pass out?

He pushed open the bathroom door. "Mara?" The room

was quiet, all the stalls empty. Dammit, where could she be? Turning around, he went back to the stables and searched, checking all the stalls and storage rooms. She wasn't here.

"Carter?" Tristan's voice carried from the arena.

Pivoting, he jogged back to the arena. The fierce frown that crossed Tristan's face when Carter exited the stables said it all. It echoed the giant, heavy pit in Carter's stomach.

"She's not back there?"

"No."

"That's her horse." Tristan pointed to the animal still trotting through the dirt.

"I know."

Cursing, Tristan took his phone from his pocket. "I'll call Gemma. Get her down here so we can gain access to the security camera feeds."

Nodding, Carter looked at Jake. "We need to catch her horse. Put him back in his stall."

Jake held up his hands. "I'm gonna leave that up to him." He pointed a finger at his partner. "I don't ride."

Tristan hung up, shaking his head. "She's on her way. I really need to get you both some lessons." He walked toward the gate and let himself into the arena. Stinger stopped and eyed him. Using a gentle tone, he moved toward the horse and snagged his reins. Tired, the animal didn't resist and followed Tristan into the stables.

Carter tried not to pace while they waited for Gemma. Instead, he put himself to work, helping Tristan unsaddle Stinger. They'd just finished putting his tack away when the rear door opened and Gemma walked in, her infant daughter, Meredith, strapped to her chest.

"Thanks for coming, Gems." Tristan held up a hand in greeting. He smiled at the baby, running a hand over his niece's dark head.

"Of course. Come on. Let's go look at the cameras. I want

to know what happened too." She tipped her head toward the main offices, then set off toward them.

The three of them, plus Maverick, followed her deeper into the building. She led them to the reception desk and sat down, logging into the computer. Carter and the others crowded in behind her as she pulled up the security cameras.

"Rewind to closing time," Tristan said. "If anyone was still here, they'd have noticed Stinger running around riderless."

Nodding, she did as he asked, then hit play. They watched Pam leave, locking the doors.

"Split the screen to show all the interior cameras. Sync them up to this point." Tristan pointed at the screen.

Gemma typed some commands into the computer. "I'm glad I learned how to work this software."

"I'm glad Ben convinced Mara to upgrade the security system," Tristan muttered.

So was Carter.

Once she had the cameras synced, Gemma hit fast-forward. Fifteen minutes after Pam left, a figure appeared at the front door.

"Slow it down." Tristan put a hand on the desk and leaned forward.

Carter did the same on her other side, and Jake leaned over her back. Gemma slowed the video down to normal speed, and they watched.

The figure hovered near the door for several moments, then the door opened and the person walked inside. They had a hood drawn over their head, obscuring their identity, but Carter could tell it was a woman.

"Dammit, she covered her face. Again." Carter sighed.

"Who is this chick?" Jake grumbled.

Gemma followed her on camera as she walked inside and went down the hallway, disappearing through the door to the arena. The cameras there were limited to the aisle that ran down the stables.

"Fast-forward again," Tristan said. "Let's see if she comes back this way or goes out the rear door."

Hitting some keys, Gemma made the video go faster. A couple minutes after she entered, they watched her come back into the main office with Mara.

Carter's heart picked up speed. He stared at Mara's face on the screen, noting the anger in her expression and in the set to her jaw.

"Come on, come on," Jake mumbled. "Show us your face."

As they neared the door, Mara looked directly at the camera. The other woman still didn't look up.

"What's she doing with her hand?" Tristan pointed at Mara on the screen.

Gemma gasped. "It's sign language."

"What?" Carter leaned closer. He didn't know she knew sign language.

"She knows a smattering because of the type of patients we see. So do I." Gemma cocked her head, watching the screen. She rewound the video, blowing up the lobby camera feed, then let it play again.

"What's it say?" Tristan asked.

"Constance. She spelled Constance." She looked at her brother.

Carter pushed away from the desk, grinding his teeth. They'd been too late to identify her. He spun back. "Is there a view of the parking lot?" Maybe they could get a view of her license plate and the kind of car she was driving.

Gemma's fingers flew over the keys as she changed the screen, then let it play. This time, Constance had parked closer, probably to limit the time people passing by saw her walking through the lot. But that meant the camera got the perfect view of her black Ford SUV and its license plate.

Tristan had his phone out before Gemma could hit pause.

Carter looked at Jake as Tristan called in the plate. "I don't like this. She's getting careless. Not only did she call from her room at the motel, but she let us see her license plate. She either intends to disappear, or not survive this. Either way, Mara's in a lot of danger."

Jake's jaw twitched, his icy blue eyes hard. He nodded once. "Agreed."

"Okay, thank you." Tristan hung up. "It's registered to a rental car company at the Asheville airport. Jake, we need to get a warrant for their records, and we need to get that finger-print evidence to the lab." Backing up a step, he patted his sister's shoulder. "Thanks, Gems. Make a copy of all that and forward it to my email, would you?"

"Already on it." Her fingers worked the keyboard.

"Carter, you coming with us?"

"Definitely." He wanted to be close in case they needed Maverick. Even if a lawyer tried to argue he shouldn't be on the case, he didn't care. If it came down to saving Mara's life or saving the case, he'd choose Mara every time.

"Good, let's go."

THIRTY-FIVE

Dark shapes flew by as they wound up the mountain road, deeper into the forest. Mara had no idea where they were going, but hopefully, they'd stop soon. The further away they got from the equestrian center, the harder it would be for Carter to find her. She'd tried to get the woman to talk, to explain what she meant about Carter killing her husband, but Constance just told her to shut up and refused to answer any of her questions. Hopefully, once they reached their destination, she'd be more willing to talk. Mara would like to know what she'd meant by that cryptic comment.

The car slowed, and Constance turned onto a dirt road. Bouncing over the rough ground, the SUV delved into the trees, finally stopping at a small, one-room cabin. Lights glowed in the front window.

"Where are we?"

"Just a little place I rented. It's better suited for my needs than my motel."

"What motel?"

Instead of answering, she opened her door. "Get out." She

pointed her gun at Mara. "But don't run. I won't hesitate to shoot you."

Eyeing the weapon warily, Mara opened her door and slid out of the vehicle. Based on the hard glint in the woman's eyes, she didn't doubt her words. Until she was alone and could escape or disarm her, Mara was stuck with the crazy bitch.

"Careful where you walk. We wouldn't want you to have an accident."

Mara's eyes widened, and she eyed the ground. "You booby-trapped this place?"

"Of course I did. It's a present for Carter when he comes to rescue you." She gave Mara a shove. "Walk."

Mouth flat as she glared at the woman, she turned her attention to the path. About halfway to the door, Constance yanked on her arm, halting her.

"Watch it."

Mara glanced down. Her foot was inches from a thin, nearly invisible wire. Gulping, she nodded and lifted her foot high, stepping over it.

At the door, Constance disabled another wire, then unlocked the door and shoved her through. "Have a seat over there." She pointed to a wooden chair by the fireplace.

Mara's eyes darted around the room as she stumbled toward the chair. A line of black, curved shields lined the center of the room, dividing it and cutting off her path to the rear door. She'd never make it before Constance could shoot her. Resigned to being captive for now, she sat down. When Constance picked up a length of rope, she stood again.

"Sit." Constance lifted the gun.

Glaring, Mara hesitated.

"I only need you breathing to get Carter here. So, if you don't want an extra hole in your body, sit down."

Gritting her teeth, Mara perched on the edge of the chair. "Fine."

Constance looped the rope around her and tugged, pulling her back in the seat. Mara wiggled her butt to sit up straighter. Slouching would just make her back hurt.

"Are you ready to tell me what this is about?" Mara turned so she could see Constance's face. "What happened? Why do you blame Carter for your husband's death?"

"Because he's responsible!" Constance yanked on the rope, pulling it tighter than was comfortable. Mara bit back a wince. "If he'd done his job correctly, Kyle would still be alive."

"I'm still confused. What did he do wrong?" Had he not investigated a case as rigorously as this woman thought he should have?

"He rushed. It's the only explanation for why he and his dog missed that mine."

Mara sucked in a breath as realization struck. "Is this about what happened in Afghanistan?"

"Ding-ding-ding. Give the woman a prize. Yes. Carter's carelessness got my husband and two others killed."

"I doubt it was carelessness." She'd heard the story from him. He'd been thorough, but he was also human. And his dog wasn't infallible. If it was even their fault.

"No. It was. Kyle would be alive if he'd done things correctly." Anger simmered in her gray-blue gaze.

Mara pressed her lips together. It wouldn't matter what she said. This woman had nurtured her hatred for years. "So, what do you intend to do?" She figured it involved killing one or both of them, but the more information she had, the better.

"Simple. Lure him here and watch him as you blow up when he trips a mine. Then he can live with the same pain I've felt for the last seven years." She pointed to Mara's chair.

Frowning, Mara glanced down. It was then that she noticed the thin wire running from both sides to the bottom of her seat. Eyes wide, she turned her gaze back to Constance. The woman grinned at her from ear-to-ear.

"You're insane."

"No." Constance bent close. "Just vindictive."

THIRTY-SIX

"Carter!" Ben's voice carried through the station.

Rolling away from his desk, Carter stood. Calling Mav, he ran through the bullpen to Ben's office. Tristan and Jake flanked the desk. Carter's eyes bounced between the three of them. "What did you find out?"

Ben nodded to Tristan.

"This." Tristan turned the tablet in his hands around and held it out to Carter. "Her prints came back."

Taking it, Carter glanced down. The name on the screen made his blood run cold.

"I take it from the lack of color in your face, you know who that is?"

Carter nodded and handed the device back to Tristan. "Constance Messer is Kyle Messer's wife. Kyle was one of the men who died after I missed an IED in a minefield in Afghanistan."

"Shit, man." Tristan's eyes were wide.

"Damn. I knew something happened to you over there." Ben shook his head.

"Yeah. It was a long time ago." He'd always feel remorseful

about what happened, but he didn't blame himself like he used to. Not after listening to Mara and seeing how his old fears affected their relationship. He was trying to do better. The first step to that was accepting that there were too many variables in what happened the day Kyle died for him to know what truly happened.

"I hate to bring back bad memories, but—"

Carter waved a hand and cut Ben off. "It's okay. What's our next move?"

"I started a warrant for her credit cards," Jake said. "Once we get that, we'll see where else she's been. Maybe we can narrow down an area where she might be holed up."

"We're working on one for her car too," Tristan added. "Hopefully, it has GPS and the rental car company can track it."

Carter nodded, but before he could say anything, his cell phone rang. Taking it from his pocket, he glanced at the screen. A local number appeared, but he didn't recognize it. His thumb hovered over the disconnect icon, but something stopped him. He looked at Ben. "Might be nothing, but—" He flashed him the screen.

Ben nodded. "Put it on speaker."

Sliding his thumb over the screen, he answered, then tapped the speakerphone icon. "This is Deputy Townsend."

"I have something of yours."

Carter's stomach sank to his toes as the woman's voice came over the line. He cleared his throat. "Excuse me?"

"Oh, don't play dumb. You might be incompetent and careless, but you aren't stupid. I know you and your colleagues raided my motel room. I also know they collected evidence and have probably run my fingerprints by now."

Surprise rounded Carter's eyes. He glanced around the room at the others, who all looked equally surprised. "How do you know that?"

"I watched. The woods around here are good for something. It's how I knew no one was minding your lady friend. How could they be when they were all at my motel room?"

Carter inhaled a shaky breath. "Is she okay? You haven't hurt her, have you?"

"She's fine for now. But it if you want her to stay that way, you need to come north. There's a rental cabin off Nine Mile Road, near Hitcher's Trail. Oh, and make sure you bring your dog. Wouldn't want to leave him out of the fun. You have an hour."

The line clicked and went silent. Carter clutched the phone, his knuckles turning white.

"You absolutely cannot go there alone." Ben pointed at him.

Anger flared to life in Carter's chest at the woman's audacity. Whatever her reasoning for targeting him, putting Mara in the middle of it was unacceptable.

"Carter. Are you listening to me?"

He turned hard eyes on Ben. "I suggest you come up with a plan quick. Because I'm walking out that door just as soon as the red fades from my vision." He pointed to the door, speaking through clenched teeth.

"Just take a breath." Ben held up a hand. "If you go there without a plan, you'll get her and yourself killed."

"I have a plan."

"Seriously? It's been thirty seconds since she hung up."

"I know you know I was EOD. That I swept for explosives with a scent detection dog. But do you know what that meant about my job in the Marines? It meant I was frequently all by myself. I learned to look out for myself. To hide and get away from insurgents without help. One crazy woman isn't going to take me out or stop me from freeing Mara."

"Let us send up a drone," Jake interjected.

"A drone?" Ben frowned.

Jake nodded and glanced at Ben, who looked interested.

"Go on, Maxwell."

"She told us where she is. If we send the drone up, it'll give us a better idea of what we're up against."

"Explosives won't show up on thermal," Carter argued.

"No, but we'll learn the lay of the cabin and the thermal scan will show us where both women are located."

"Can you do it in the time allotted?" Ben asked.

"So long as it doesn't take us too long to get there. I'm not familiar with where that is."

"It's about a forty-minute drive. Thirty if we push it," Tristan said.

"Why did she give us so much time if that's all the longer it takes?" Carter's mind cycled through possible reasons. None of them were good. All of them involved some sort of ambush.

"I don't know, but I'm not looking a gift-horse in the mouth. Jake, go get the drone. Meet us in the parking lot. Tristan, go get the comm equipment." Ben barked orders as he came around his desk. "Carter, let's go arm ourselves." He led the charge out the door, where they all split in different directions.

Carter followed him to the armory, but before they walked in, he turned into the room where they kept the SWAT equipment.

"What are you looking for?"

"Bomb defusing stuff." He knew there wasn't much, but SWAT carried some tools he could repurpose.

Ben nodded. "I'm going to get the rifles." He was gone from view before Carter could acknowledge him.

Digging into the lockers, Carter rooted through the equipment. They kept some basic stuff on hand, but he wished he had the full kit he used to carry.

His hands paused on the crate he'd just tipped forward to

look into. He still had most of his old gear. It was in the closet with the pictures Mara found.

A quick glance at his watch made him grimace. They'd already wasted five minutes. His house was on the right side of town for where they needed to go, but it was a couple of minutes off the main drag. With the time it would take him to get inside and get all the gear, they'd be pushing it.

But the gear he had was better than anything he'd find here. He wanted to be prepared, even if he didn't use any of it.

Shoving the crate back onto the shelf, he shut the locker. It was worth the risk. He opened another locker and took out the flexible camera SWAT used. This, though, he didn't have.

"Ben." Jogging down the hall, he stopped as the sheriff emerged from the armory holding two rifles and a small duffel, which Carter presumed was full of ammo.

"What's up?"

"We need to stop at my house. I have all my old gear still stored away. I need my kit."

"You're sure you know where it is? We don't have much time."

"I'm sure."

Ben gave a short nod. "Go. One of us will drop you a pin to the location." His expression hardened. "If you beat us there, you wait, or so help me, I'll throw your ass in jail for obstruction when this is all over."

Carter knew he was serious, but he didn't care. If he got there and discovered an imminent threat to Mara's life, he was going in whether he had backup or not. But he nodded anyway. "Will do. See you there." Spinning on his heel, he called for Maverick and dashed out of the station. Stowing his dog in the back, he climbed into the car and pulled out of the lot, lights and sirens going.

At his house, he hit the end of the driveway hard, rocking the car. Maverick's nails scrabbled on the metal kennel flooring. "Sorry, bud." Braking hard, he stopped in the middle of the drive and got out. The dog barked, clearly confused, but Carter just locked the doors and ran for the house. Letting himself inside, he made a beeline for the closet where he'd hidden all his old gear in a box at the back. He yanked open the doors and pulled everything out. His hands shook as he opened the flaps and reached inside for the backpack he hadn't touched in almost seven years.

Knowing it contained everything he needed, he didn't open it. Just stood and ran back to his cruiser. Maverick continued to bark as he buckled up. "I know. Hold on. We'll get moving again soon." He picked up his phone, checking for the pin Ben said they'd drop. Finding it, he enabled the directions and backed out of the driveway.

Miles ticked by, the scenery flashing blue and red as he made his way through the mountains to Nine Mile Road. When he turned onto it, it was nothing more than a dirt track.

Cutting his lights, he slowed. Headlights appeared in his rearview mirror, and he pulled off to the side. As the vehicle approached, he realized it was another county cruiser. The car drove up next to him, and he rolled down his window. It was Ben.

"Tristan and Jake are right behind me." He hooked a thumb over his shoulder.

Carter glanced in his rearview mirror and saw more headlights.

"Jake's going to send the drone up. We've still got ten minutes."

Edginess filled Carter. That wasn't a lot of time. "Tell him to hurry. I want time to get past anything she's rigged up."

Ben nodded and put his vehicle in park, getting out. In moments, Jake had a small black drone out of the rear of the car and in the air.

The three of them crowded around him, watching the

image on the screen attached to the remote he held. It whisked above the treetops, quickly locating the cabin and Constance's car. Jake brought the drone lower and confirmed her license plate, then circled the house. Carter took note of the doors and their lack of outside lighting. It would be harder to see, but it also meant she would have a harder time seeing him.

"You see any cameras?" Ben asked.

"Not on the main building." Jake lofted the drone and flew it over to the small shed at the rear of the property. It, too, looked devoid of electronics.

"Switch to thermal," Carter said. He wanted to know where they were, and if it was just Constance they were dealing with, or if she'd roped someone else into her scheme.

The screen changed, and a gradient of blues and greens appeared. Except in the main room of the cabin. There, two bright red, people-shaped blobs appeared. One was moving, the other stationary. Jake surveyed the shed as well as the immediate area around the cabin, but they only saw the two heat signatures.

"I've seen enough. Let's go." Carter walked around to the passenger side of his vehicle and removed the backpack he grabbed from his house. When he shut the door, the others stood near the hood of his car.

"You guys can follow, but don't get close. Ben, I know this is your show, but none of you have experience with land mines and IEDs."

The sheriff held up his hands. "By all means, lead us in."

Tristan held up an ear piece, small microphone, and battery pack. "Put this on."

Carter took the comm unit and donned it. "Are we ready?"

The others nodded. Carter took a step toward the rear of his vehicle and opened the kennel door. Maverick jumped down and barked.

"Mav, *ruhig*."

Immediately, the dog quieted. Carter snapped the leash to his harness. "*Fuss*."

Together, he and Mav made their way up the lane. Carter trained his eyes on the ground, sweeping the road with his flashlight. With where Constance's car was parked, he figured the road to that point was clear, but he wasn't taking any chances. She could have put mines where the car wheels didn't travel.

They made it to the rear of the Ford SUV without incident, and he flicked off his light. He pressed the mic button on his comm. "Clear to the vehicle. Don't enter the yard."

Ben's quiet affirmative came through the earpiece.

Keeping Mav tucked close, Carter edged his way past the car, using the moonlight as a guide and praying it was enough. Constance would see his flashlight if she looked out the front window, so he couldn't use it. Watching every foot placement either of them made, they circled the cabin, staying in the shadows close to the tree line, and came up from the rear.

He repeated the commands for Mav to heel and to stay quiet, then slowly advanced. Back here, with the only window set into the back door, he chanced the flashlight. About twenty feet from the door, it glinted off a fine filament hovering just above the grass.

She was good. If he hadn't been looking, he wouldn't have seen it. Checking the ground beyond, he noted it running toward the house before he lost it in the low light. Carter grabbed the handle on Maverick's vest and lifted the dog over the wire, carrying him a few feet before setting him down. He located the filament again and followed it to where it snaked under the door.

Carter let out a soft curse. There was no telling if the wire was hooked to a mine on the door, or if it was a decoy meant to scare him into going around front. Or knocking.

Backing up a few feet, he activated his mic. "I'm at the back door. It's booby-trapped." He crouched, opening the backpack to retrieve the small camera he took from the SWAT equipment room.

"Don't go in." Ben's voice was stern in his ear.

"I'm using the snake." Unfolding the camera, he turned it on and threaded the scope under the door, leaving it flush with the frame as he looked around. Mara sat tied to a chair near the fireplace. Constance paced, avoiding the windows, but stopping at the edge to look out.

He pressed his mic again. "Stay in the shadows. She's watching out the front window."

"Copy."

Turning the thin cable, he found the filament. It wasn't fixed to the door. Instead, it ran along the floor through a series of eye bolts and under Mara's chair.

"Shit," he whispered. His heart jumped into his throat. Mara was sitting on a mine. He pressed the button on his mic. They needed a better plan.

THIRTY-SEVEN

Mara's eyes tracked Constance as she paced. Back and forth, she went from the kitchen area to the window and back, pausing about every third or fourth pass to look out the window. She didn't know what the woman was hoping to see. Mara doubted Carter would announce himself, even with the time limit Constance gave him.

Only the gun pressed to her temple had kept Mara quiet during that conversation. She hadn't wanted to give Carter a reason to barge in without a care to his own safety. If Constance hit her or shot her to keep her quiet, he wouldn't care what happened to him. He was already angry. She'd heard the steel in his voice, even from a distance.

Glancing away, she shifted in her seat, pulling against the ropes binding her to the chair. With a sigh, she dropped her gaze. Something near the floor at the back door caught her eye. She squinted, then quickly schooled her features as Constance turned. Putting on a blank mask, she looked around the room again, taking in the ballistic plates set up in a line. Constance wasn't dumb. She knew what would happen if the mine under Mara's chair went off before she was out of the cabin. She'd stayed on the other side of the plates since she tied Mara to the seat. It left Mara feeling bleak. If the mine tripped, she wondered if she'd even know.

But that little movement she glimpsed at the door gave her hope.

As soon as Constance turned her back to the door, Mara let her gaze drop to the floor. A small black cable reappeared from beneath the door. It was a camera scope. While she watched, it rotated, pointing up, then went slowly from one side of the doorframe to the other; retreating one more time as Constance turned around.

Mara's heart rate soared. It had to be Carter. Did he realize she was strapped to a mine? Had he seen the superfine wire leading inside to her chair?

Constance paced back to the window, pausing again to look out. Mara took the opportunity to sign the word bomb and prayed he saw it.

"Your boyfriend is about to be late."

Mara lowered her hand, rolling her wrist to hide any movements Constance might have seen. "He'll be here."

Constance walked toward her, coming up to the very edge of the ballistic shield. "Maybe he needs more incentive." She lifted her phone and her gun. "Maybe hearing you scream as I put a bullet in you will help."

The phone rang in her hand.

"Lucky, lucky." Constance lowered the gun and answered, putting it on speaker. "I was about to make you hurry."

"I'm here. Let her go. It's me you want."

Constance laughed. "Not hardly. I want you to suffer. Like I've suffered." Twin pops of color erupted on her face. "Walk up here."

"Do you have a death wish? I know you booby-trapped this place. At this distance, shrapnel will come through the windows if I trip something."

Mara opened her mouth to warn him about the mine under her seat, but Constance raised her gun, eyeing her with a hard look.

"I'll be fine." She stroked her shirt, which was lumpy from the vest she wore beneath. Come to the front door. "You brought your dog, right?"

"Yes."

"Good." She hung up, a cold smile spreading over her face. "Time for lover-boy to face his past." She walked to the door, standing to the side.

A soft knock echoed through the silence a minute later. Reaching out, Constance turned the doorknob, and the door swung in with a creak. Mara's heartbeat quickened as Carter came into view. Unarmed, he still looked lethal. His silvery eyes were hard as he locked his gaze on Constance.

Bile rose in Mara's throat as the reality of what was happening hit her. Someone in the next few minutes would likely end up seriously hurt or dead.

"Step inside and shut the door." Constance stepped back, pointing her gun in Mara's direction.

Carter did as she asked. Maverick growled at her. She swung her weapon around and trained it on the dog. He barked and took a step forward.

"*Nein. Sitz,*" Carter ordered.

Maverick's butt hit the floor, but he continued to growl.

"So well-trained. It's nice to see you've learned since the last one."

Carter's face stayed an emotionless mask except for the quick twitch in his jaw. Mara knew Constance had struck a nerve.

"Put the gun down, Constance. Let's talk."

"We can talk like this." Her aim stayed on Maverick.

"Fine. Fill in some holes for me. You were behind all the vandalism? And the tear gas?"

She nodded.

"How did you get your hands on that stuff? And the mine you used at Mara's? It's not like you can walk into an army surplus store and buy those."

"Well, after you got my husband killed, I spent years planning my revenge. I cultivated friendships with some influential and knowledgeable people. They got me everything I needed. Including the fake check I used to get into Mara's good graces." She glanced at Mara, then turned back to Carter. "You know, your relationship was rather fortuitous. I've been following your movements for a few months, waiting for the right time to pay your mother a visit, when Mara entered the picture. It was like fate handed me a present wrapped in a pretty bow."

Mara rolled her eyes. The woman was crazy. But smart. She still didn't know what Carter's plan was to get them out of this. She hoped he had one. Because she didn't. Her immediate goal was to get off this chair. She squirmed against the ropes.

"I get that you're angry. But what happened was an accident. No one knows exactly what happened. I checked that entire section of road and a hundred meters out in every direction. It's possible Bob missed it, yes. But it's also possible the insurgents came back after I searched, saw all my flags and added a few more mines and IEDs just to screw with us."

Constance let out a mirthless laugh. "No. It's your fault. Yours and that damn dog's." Her gaze traveled to Maverick, who still sat by Carter's side, giving the woman a low growl. "Why anyone would trust an animal is beyond me. They're stupid. I don't care how well they can smell. It doesn't replace human eyes or modern equipment. Maybe if you'd been out there with a metal detector, you'd have found the mine."

"Actually, a lot of what I found wasn't metal. It was plastic bottles filled with chemical agents. A metal detector wouldn't have helped much."

Her face turned bright red. She took a quick step toward Carter. Maverick scooted forward several inches, barking, and she froze.

"Make him lie down."

Carter held her gaze, but did as she asked. "Mav, *platz*."

Still barking, the dog lowered to the ground.

"Perfect. Now make sure he stays there." She walked over to the fireplace and picked up a roll of duct tape off the mantle. "Hold up your hands." Tucking it under her arm, she peeled the tape free of the roll.

Mara watched Carter's jaw twitch. His hands curled into fists, and he slowly raised them. Constance came out from behind the shield, and with quick movements—all while keeping her gun trained on Mara—she wrapped the tape around his wrists. She tucked the roll under her arm again and severed the tape, then tore off a shorter piece.

"Tell your dog to stay."

Eyes never leaving their captor, Carter complied. "Maverick, *bleib*."

That mirthless smile returning to her face, she stepped closer to Carter and slapped the tape over his mouth. "Go behind the shield." She gestured to the plates separating the room.

He grunted and shook his head. Constance raised an eyebrow, readjusting her grip on her gun, which was still pointed at Mara. "I can make her death painful."

Mara sucked in a breath and held it. She didn't want that. She didn't want to die at all, but she didn't see how she could get out of this. Carter was bound and unable to command Maverick. She was bound to this damn chair. And Constance had a gun.

Carter let out a grunt and stomped across the floor and

around the barrier. Constance followed. Maverick's barks resumed a fevered pitch, but he stayed on the floor.

"Sit." Constance pointed to another wooden chair.

Carter sat. Despair made Mara's chest ache. Tears pressed against her eyes and spilled free. Anguish filled Carter's silvery eyes as he stared at her.

"I love you," she mouthed.

A single tear slid from Carter's eye a moment before his expression changed. His eyes hardened with a fierce determination. His gaze flicked to Maverick and back.

Mara frowned and glanced at the dog. His dark eyes were focused on his handler, waiting for his next command.

Carter grunted. Mara looked at him. Again, he glanced at the dog, then back at her. Her eyes grew round as she realized what he was trying to tell her. He wasn't the only one to whom the dog listened.

"You know, it's a shame I won't be here to witness your anguish as she and your dog die. I just can't take that chance. Being in the same room while we waited on you was chance enough. Part of me hoped you'd trip the mine as you came up. But I also had a feeling you'd be too smart for that. I can't have an injury slow me down, though. Your friends are probably out there somewhere, just waiting."

He grunted again as she walked around behind him and held up the tape roll. Mara realized she planned to tape him to the chair.

Using her teeth, Constance peeled the tape back, but when she tried to secure it to him, it wouldn't stay stuck to him when she pulled to wrap it around his torso. With a huff, she tucked her gun into her waistband.

Mara didn't hesitate. She wouldn't get another chance. "Maverick, *fass!*"

The dog shot off the floor like a coiled spring. He leapt over the shield, landed beside Carter, and had Constance's arm in his mouth in less than a second. The woman screamed and reached for her gun.

Carter stood and whirled, grabbing her free hand. Bending it behind her back, he forced her to her knees. Maverick held onto her other arm. Constance still screamed.

Mara searched her brain for the command to release the dog. What was it? Ow? Owl? "Maverick, *aus*!" The dog let go and backed up several steps. Bent low, he barked in her face, warning her he'd bite her again.

Forcing Constance onto her belly, Carter straddled her back, then reached up with his bound hands and yanked the tape off his face. "Good boy, Mav. Good boy. *Pass auf*."

The dog's muscles tensed and his barks shifted to a low growl as Carter told him to guard. His eyes never left Constance.

With his teeth, Carter found the edge of the tape on his wrists and yanked. Circling his hands, he pulled, unraveling it until he could separate his fists. Once free, he reached for the handcuffs on the back of his utility belt and secured them around Constance's wrists.

Mara's breath left her on a whoosh as relief flooded over her like a fifty-gallon drum of water. Then the tears came. She was vaguely aware of Carter pulling a thin wire from his pocket and pressing a button on it. His low voice carried over the sound of Constance blubbering about her arm as he spoke to someone outside. A moment later, he was in front of her.

"Hey, baby. Let's get you free."

She gave a jerky nod and inhaled a breath through her nose, trying to calm herself. "Yes, please."

He pulled a folded knife from his pocket and flicked it open. The rope around her chest loosened as he cut through it, then fell away.

"Stay put for a minute." Carter put his hands on her shoulders when she would have dove into him. "I want to look at the mine under you before you get up. Make sure she didn't attach a secondary trigger to you."

"I don't think she did, unless there was something already on the chair when I sat down."

He nodded and bent low to look under the seat. Mara craned her neck to see what he was doing. His fingers traced the thin wires running from under the chair to the doors.

"It looks like it's just the two she's got strung up that go outside. I should be able to cut them and it'll be fine. My tools are outside, though."

"Okay. Can I get up?"

"Not yet. Let me go get my bag. I want to remove the mine first." He patted her knee and stood, disappearing out the front door for a moment, then coming back with a khaki-colored backpack. Opening it, he withdrew a set of wire cutters.

Mara squeezed her eyes shut. She'd rather not see them get blown to smithereens.

A soft snick reached her ears over the sound of Constance crying on the other side of the ballistic plates. Then another. When nothing happened, Mara opened one eye. "Is it safe?"

He glanced at her, then chuckled. "You're fine."

"Can I get up now?"

"Not yet." He reached into his bag and came out with a small battery-powered screwdriver. "I want to take this thing off the chair. She attached it with brackets." His head dipped again.

Mara heard the soft whir of the screwdriver and felt the vibrations through the chair. In less than a minute, he sat back, the device in his hands.

"I'm going to take this outside." He stood and walked away.

Mara's shoulders sagged, and she pressed a hand to her chest as the adrenaline dump left her weak.

Carter's boots thudded across the floor, then he was in front of her. His face filled her vision, and she launched herself at him. He caught her and rolled back on his heels to sit on the floor, hauling her into his lap. She let the tears flow as she clung to him.

"I'm so sorry, Mara." He buried his hands in her hair. "I'm sorry she came after you. I love you. So much."

Pulling back, she sniffed. "I love you too. And don't be sorry. This wasn't your fault. She's just a crazy bitch."

He huffed a laugh and leaned in to press a kiss to her lips.

Male voices floated to her ears, then suddenly, they weren't alone anymore. Ben, Tristan, and Jake entered the small cabin. Carter lifted his head and sat back to point to the ballistic plates.

"She's back there." He moved Mara off his lap and stood. "Maverick, *hier*."

With a final, short bark, the dog trotted around the plates to Carter's side. Jake and Tristan took his place and lifted Constance off the floor.

"He bit me! That fucking dog bit me!" Constance jerked against their hold, glaring at Maverick.

"You'll be all right." Tristan pushed her toward the door. "We'll call an ambulance to look at you."

Shouting obscenities, Constance continued to twist in Tristan's hold as he and Jake ushered her from the cabin.

"For the record, your plan failed." Ben crossed his arms and lifted an eyebrow as he stared at Carter.

"There was a plan?" Mara asked. "What was the plan?"

"To send Maverick in and take her down. But then she threatened to shoot you because I was taking too long to show up, and the plan went up in smoke."

"We did get her entire confession, though. That part of your plan worked."

Mara sent a questioning frown at them both.

Carter held up the comm unit. "I set it to an open channel before I came in so they could hear what was happening. They recorded everything she said."

A bright smile covered Mara's face. "Good. She'll rot in jail for a long time."

"Not as long as I'd like, but yes. She'll be there for a good ten years."

Maverick nudged Mara's hand. She looked down and smiled at the dog, then crouched to give him a hug. "The plan sort of worked. He did take her down." She framed his face, scratching the sides of his ears. "Didn't you, boy? You were a good boy. You listened so well."

"I still can't believe that worked." Ben shook his head. "Someone knows Mara's family."

Carter crouched next to Mara and put a hand on the dog's head. "Yeah." He looked at Mara. "He knows."

EPILOGUE

The seatbelt pressed into Carter's chest as he braked hard in front of his house. What were all these cars doing here? He recognized Mara's SUV, but Tristan's truck was also parked out front, along with several others.

He squinted at the small blue SUV in the drive. And was that his mom's car?

Turning into the drive, he parked behind it and got out. Still frowning, he walked up the front porch steps and let himself inside.

"Surprise!" A chorus of voices greeted him.

Carter blinked, taking in the people in his living room. "What is going on?"

With a bright smile on her face, Mara stepped forward. "Happy birthday."

A wrinkle formed on his forehead. "My birthday was last month."

"I know. But in the chaos that surrounded Constance's arrest, we didn't celebrate." She shrugged. "Your mom wanted to come visit anyway. And I figured it was a good way to announce to all our friends that I've moved in."

He rolled his eyes. "Everyone knew that already."

She smacked his chest. "Stop bursting my bubble and enjoy the party."

Laughing, he leaned down and pressed a kiss to her forehead. "Yes, ma'am."

The door opened behind him, and Ben stepped through, smiling.

Carter narrowed his eyes at his boss and friend. "You knew about this, didn't you?"

Ben's smile widened. "Who do you think came up with the idea to get you out of the house? Without your dog." He pointed at the Malinois, who sported a party hat.

He glanced at the dog, and his eyes widened. "Oh, geez. What are you wearing? I'm so sorry, Mav."

Mara giggled. "He likes it."

"He does not. He's a badass police dog. They don't wear party hats. And they certainly don't like them."

She hummed and lifted an eyebrow.

Grinning, Carter waded into the room and found his mom. She was talking to Tristan's wife, Laurel, and holding their son, Wyatt.

"Hi, sweetie."

"Hey, Mom." He enfolded her in a hug, baby and all. "Thanks for coming."

"Of course." She kissed his cheek, then peered past him at Mara. "I like your girlfriend even better in person. She's bold, like you. And hard to say no to. Mara called me out of the blue last week and asked me to come out for a visit. She was very persuasive."

They'd had several video chats between the three of them in the last month. Carter knew Mara and his mom were getting along great, but he had no idea they'd become so buddy-buddy behind his back. "You still could have said no."

She gave him a look that said he was crazy. "And miss this?" She gestured around the room. "Or this?" Tilting an elbow, she raised the baby in her arms. "Speaking of, when do I get one of these from you?"

Carter patted her shoulder with a chuckle. "Slow down, Mom. We've got time."

She let out a little snort. "Not that much." She shook a finger at him. "Don't take too long. You never know how quick it'll happen."

Sobering at the reminder of her infertility issues and the reason he was an only child, he nodded. "I'll keep that in mind."

"Good. Now, introduce me to some of these people. They've all arrived in the last ten minutes or so, and I only know a few."

Smile returning, he led her around the room. One person he was surprised to see was Agent Porter. Pausing next to the man, who stood with Jake and the local coroner Cullen Tate and his fiancée Piper Riordan, Carter held out a hand. "Thanks for coming, Agent Porter."

"Call me Finn, please. And I'm glad to be here. I was in town to talk to Ben, and he suggested I swing by." He shrugged. "I'm not one to pass up cake, so here I am."

"Cake? Mara didn't tell me there was cake." Carter looked at his mom. "Is there cake?"

"What's a birthday party without cake?" A wicked smile crossed her face. "I brought the candles."

Carter laughed. "I hope Mara invited someone from the fire department."

Hands snaked around his waist. He raised an arm as Mara ducked under it.

"Don't worry, hon. There's a fire extinguisher under the sink."

Smiling down at her, he held her close. "You sure you're okay tying yourself to such an old man?"

A sweet smile settled over her features. "Yeah. He's a pretty great old man. And I love him."

Carter lowered his head. "He loves you too."

Thank you for reading Smoky Mountain K-9! I hope you enjoyed it. Please consider leaving a rating or review on Amazon and/or Goodreads. It would be greatly appreciated! If you'd like a FREE romantic suspense novella just for signing up and EXCLUSIVE looks twice a month at my latest work-in-progress, you can join my mailing list at ashleyaquinn.com. You can also stay up-to-date on my newest projects by joining my Facebook readers' group, Ashley's She Shed. See you next time!

~

Keep reading for a sneak peek at Book 6 in the Foggy Mountain Intrigue series, Smoky Mountain Judge.

Smoky Mountain Judge

FOGGY MOUNTAIN
BOOK 6

ONE

"Pax!" Kennedy Davidson stood at the end of the hallway, yelling toward the stairs from the kitchen for her son. She let out a long breath as she looked up, praying for patience. "Come on. We're going to be late. It's your first day. Your sister is already in the car."

Heavy footsteps thudded on the stairs, and a moment later, her tall, lanky fifteen-year-old rounded the banister, backpack slung over one shoulder. A lock of his wavy light brown hair fell over his forehead. He tossed his head, getting it out of his eyes.

"You ready?" Kennedy raised an eyebrow as he walked toward her.

"I guess." He marched past her into the kitchen, snagging the breakfast sandwich she made for him off the counter as he headed toward the door.

Kennedy rolled her eyes. One day soon, they were going to have a "Come to Jesus" type talk about his attitude, but not today. Not when they were already running behind on the first day of school—at a new school.

Snagging her purse and lunch sack from the counter, she

followed him out the door into the garage, where they piled into the car.

"You're worse than a girl." Pax's twin sister, Paige, pinned her brother with a dry look.

"Shut up."

"Hey." Kennedy glanced in the mirror. "Can we please not fight? Today's supposed to be exciting. It's a new start for all of us." She didn't want to start her new job as a magistrate judge for the federal district court stressed out because her kids were at each other's throats. One morning without an argument was all she was asking for.

Paxton rolled his eyes and looked out the window. Paige gave her mother a naughty smile, but stayed silent.

Thanking her lucky stars they'd listened, Kennedy opened the garage door and started the engine. Sunshine streamed inside. It was a nice change from the dreariness of the last several days. Spring had arrived and brought rain with it.

"Everyone have everything?" She glanced in the back.

"Yes," Paige said.

Paxton nodded, now focused on his food.

"Good." Kennedy pulled out of the garage.

The ride to the kids' school was short. When she'd looked for houses in Asheville, she'd restricted the area so she wouldn't have to get on the highway to take the kids to school. It was bad enough she'd have to use it to get to work. Driving was not her favorite pastime.

Turning off the main road, she joined the line of cars in the drop-off zone. When they were within a few car lengths of the doors, she glanced back. "Do you guys remember where you're going?"

Pax rolled his eyes and reached for the door handle.

"We'll be good, Mom." Paige opened her door. "See you this evening."

"Okay. Have a good day."

Paige waved, but Pax just got out, shutting his door without a backward glance.

Blowing out a breath, Kennedy shook her head. She knew this move would be hard. Especially with only a few weeks left of the school year. Her appointment to the court was terrible timing, but it was an opportunity she couldn't say no to. Especially when it brought her closer to her oldest brother and his family. And away from her useless ex-husband and her overbearing mother.

Back on the main road, Kennedy headed for the interstate loop to take her downtown. At least the federal building wasn't far off the interstate. She was not sorry to get away from the congestion in Richmond. Hoping her drive would be easy, she turned on her radio, searching for a traffic report as she merged onto the interstate. Song after song greeted her until an announcer's voice droned over the speakers.

"An accident on two-forty just north of Tunnel Road has slowed things down for eastbound traffic."

Kennedy frowned. She wasn't sure where that was. But she was traveling westbound, so hopefully, things were clear for her. Listening to the rest of the report, the announcer said nothing else of note, so she changed the station to one with music. She hummed along as she drove, soon exiting the morning rush and weaving her way through the surface streets to the federal building. Parking in the staff lot, she grabbed her things and headed inside, glad she'd come in late last week to get her security badge and orient herself to her surroundings. Today would go much more smoothly with all the admin stuff out of the way.

After passing through security, she took the elevator to the office suite she shared with her new boss. Excitement fluttered in her veins as she paused outside the door. She'd been a judge at the local level for several years. A lawyer for several more before that. But this was a different playing field. One day, she wanted to be the one on the other side of the door waiting for her new magistrate to arrive.

"You got this. Rock your new role," she muttered to herself. Extending a hand, she grasped the knob and turned it, stepping inside.

Chaos greeted her. Two law clerks scurried from desk to desk, while behind the central reception area, sat an older woman with a deep frown between her eyebrows and a phone receiver tucked into her shoulder. Kennedy learned last week that Suzie MacKinnon ran a tight ship. If there was this much chaos, something was wrong.

Suzie glanced up as Kennedy walked in, her expression morphing to one of relief. Murmuring into the phone, she hung it up. "Oh, thank God you're here."

"What? Why? What's wrong?"

"Judge Jedynak was in an accident on his way to work. We're trying to figure out which cases we can reschedule or pass off to another district judge and which ones you can handle."

The announcer's report echoed through her mind. She hoped the judge's accident wasn't serious. "Okay. Let me put my things in my office, and I'll help you." Her feet were already moving toward her office door. She found the key on her keyring and unlocked it. Inside, she dumped her stuff on her desk, then turned around and pushed up her sleeves. So much for an easy first day.

Two

An edginess skated along Finley Porter's spine as he walked out of the courtroom. That hearing didn't go the way he expected. Gustavo Herrera's attorney was like a piranha, devouring every statement, every thing in his path. Finn wanted to see the drug lord put away for a long, long time. He thought they'd built a solid case, but much of it hinged on Piper Riordan's testimony, and the defense counsel was out for blood. The man had latched onto her background, and was attempting to make her sound forgetful and lazy, which called her suitability as a witness into question. Thankfully, she wasn't there to hear him berate her character. At least the judge dismissed the motion to suppress her testimony. It didn't bode well for the trial, though. Finn was glad Piper had thick skin. She would need it when Herrera's attorney cross-examined her.

"Porter!"

Finn paused, glancing back. Another federal prosecutor, Joe Caster, walked toward him.

"I wondered if I'd see you here today." Joe stopped several feet away and held out a hand.

"Yeah." Finn shook it. "Wilkins asked me to be here. To give my impression of his main witness." He'd stayed up late, prepping for today, but even with that, Herrera's attorney still surprised him.

"He told me about that after I overheard him on the phone with her. She was ticked there was even a question about whether she'd be allowed to testify." Joe shook his head, one corner of his mouth kicking up.

An answering smile lifted one side of Finn's lips. "Yeah, she's a firecracker. It's why she's still alive." Piper's unwillingness to give in and let Herrera win saved her life. "You didn't stop me, though, to talk about Wilkins' case. What's up?"

Joe sobered. "I figured talking to you now would save me an email. I need everything you've got on Javy Gonzales."

Finn frowned. "Javy Gonzales? Why?" He'd been chasing the mid-level drug boss for over a year as part of the task force trying to take down the Vargas-Ruiz cartel. But he didn't think they were close to arresting him yet. They didn't have enough evidence on any of the charges they were pursuing.

"I just came from his bail hearing with Judge Davidson. It was denied. Now I need to review all the evidence and build my case."

"Bail hearing? When was he arrested? And for what? By whom?" Finn reached into his pocket for his phone to check his email, then remembered it was in his office since he couldn't have it in court. Clenching his teeth, he pierced Caster with a stare.

"Wait, you didn't know? The DEA brought him in yesterday on federal drug trafficking charges. They caught him in a sting they did."

Finn's frown deepened. Why hadn't Sharpe told him about this? They'd been working to bring Gonzales in on not just drugs, but on illegal firearms sales too. Gonzales' little operation was funneling weapons to other cartel sects and terrorist groups around the country.

"I'll have to get back to you on that. I need to talk to Nick and find out what happened. And who's Judge Davidson?" That was not a name he was familiar with.

"She's Judge Jedynak's new magistrate. Seemed competent. But she ruled in my favor. Ask me again when she shoots me down."

Finn chuckled. "True. But, hey, thanks for the heads-up. I'll talk to Nick and get back to you."

"Sounds good." With a wave, Caster walked off.

Smile fading, Finn's frown returned. He bit the corner of his mouth, glancing back at the direction Caster came from. Why didn't Sharpe let him know about Gonzales' arrest?

His feet carried him down the corridor. He doubted Nick was on this side of the complex; Caster would have mentioned it. But maybe he could catch a glimpse of Gonzales and get a sense of his mood. The man was a cocky bastard, but if Sharpe's team had him dead to rights, he might feel a little deflated. That could give Finn the in he needed to get some information out of the man. He wanted him to roll on Herrera, but that was likely wishful thinking. It would take more than a few trafficking charges to get Gonzales to turn on his boss. No, he'd need to prove weapons charges too. Unless Nick had something extra-juicy on the guy.

Finn's shoes scuffed softly on the marble floors, the sound echoing off the walls as he moved down the corridor. It was probably a video hearing—if Gonzales was even required to attend. The defendant didn't always have to appear for discovery hearings. Mouth flattening, Finn picked up the pace. On the off-chance it wasn't, he wanted to catch a glimpse of him.

At a quick clip, he soon reached the area where Jedynak's

magistrates held court. A quick scan of the hallway revealed no one of note, but defendants went out another door.

Which he didn't have access to.

Biting back a groan, Finn pressed the heels of his hands to his eyes. He needed sleep. All his late nights lately were catching up with him.

"You okay, Agent Porter?"

Finn lowered his hands and looked at the court officer standing outside one of the rooms, recognizing him. "Hey, Shawn." He gave the younger man a polite smile. "Yeah, I'm fine. Just tired."

"I hear that. Do you know how little newborns sleep? I thought I did. Then I had one." He shook his head. "I don't remember what it's like to sleep all night."

Chuckling, Finn walked closer. "You got new pictures?" He'd seen some right after Shawn's son was born, but none since. Finn liked kids, so he didn't mind when his colleagues showed off new pictures.

"Not on me." Shawn shook his head. "My phone's in my locker." His expression changed, and he gave Finn a small frown. "What are you doing over this way, anyway? I heard Herrera had a hearing today, but it's not over here."

"I actually just came from it. I ran into Joe Caster on my way out. He said the DEA arrested someone I've had my eye on. I wanted to see if I could catch a glimpse of him. Gauge his mood. He's got information I want."

"Ah. I think you're out of luck on that front. All the hearings are video conferences today."

The doors behind him opened, and several people filed out. Finn glanced inside, his eyes pausing on the woman behind the bench. "That the new judge?"

Shawn nodded. "Poor woman got thrown into the fire today."

Finn frowned, turning away from the dark-haired, bespectacled woman in black robes. "What do you mean?"

"It's her first day of actual hearings, and Judge Jedynak was in a bad car accident on the way into work this morning. She's had to take on extra work."

"What? Oh, man. Is he okay?" Finn wasn't going to ask how Shawn knew all this. He'd learned the court officers knew everything.

"Not sure. All I've heard was it was bad. He's alive, but I don't know the extent of his injuries."

"Damn. Well, I hope he's all right." He liked Robert Jedynak. The man was fair in his rulings and knew the law backwards and forwards. It kept Finn on his toes and made him be a better agent; he didn't want his cases to get tossed because he didn't follow the correct procedures.

"Me too."

Finn took one more look at the woman at the head of the courtroom before the door swung shut behind the last person. She didn't look frazzled. She looked in control.

And sexy in those dark-framed glasses.

Whoa. Finn shifted on his feet. Where did that thought come from? Gritting his teeth, he took a step away and glanced at Shawn. "Hey, thanks for the info on Jedynak. I'll see you later." He backed up, then pointed a finger at the man. "Print out some new pictures and carry them around. I want to see how Aidan's changed."

Shawn smiled. "Will do. Go get some sleep."

Oh, if only he could. He still had a full day ahead of him. "I'll try."

Grinning, a knowing look entered Shawn's eyes. "Cuppa makes a strong Americano." He winked, referencing the coffee shop around the corner.

Finn returned his smile. "Oh, I know." Backing away, he lifted a hand in farewell, then turned, heading back the way he came. He'd definitely hit up the coffee shop at some point today. They kept a coffeepot in the office, but even with as strong as they made it, it didn't match what he could get at Cuppa. Nor did it taste as good.

But first, he wanted answers. Nick had some explaining to do.

Bypassing the ATF offices, he wandered up a floor to the DEA's offices. Finn stepped off the elevator and went down the hall, his stride purposeful. He supposed he probably should have called ahead first to see if Sharpe was even in his office, but his impulse control was in short supply thanks to his lack of sleep.

Finn stopped outside Nick's door and rapped his knuckles on it. A low voice on the other side told him to enter. He twisted the doorknob and stepped into the opening.

Nick's expression turned apologetic when he saw Finn, and he held up a hand. "I know. I'm sorry. Things happened quick yesterday. I didn't realize who we had until we had him. Once we had everyone processed, I went home and crashed. I was going to catch you later this morning. How'd you find out, anyway?"

"Joe Caster." Finn strolled in, shutting the door, and sat down. "We met in the hallway. He asked me for what I had on the guy. He's been denied bail, by the way."

Nick's head bobbed. "Good. That should give us enough time to gather more evidence on the other charges we want to throw at him. I'm glad Jedynak saw things our way. I was afraid he'd discount Gonzales' ties to Herrera."

"Jedynak wasn't the one who denied bail. He was in a car wreck this morning. It was his new magistrate."

"Oh?" Nick's dark brows furrowed over his brown eyes. "He okay?"

Finn lifted one shoulder. "Don't know. It was nasty from what I heard. Hopefully, we'll hear more soon."

"Yeah, hopefully. Damn. That throws a wrench into things. They'll have to postpone a bunch of stuff if he's going to be out for a while. The magistrates can only do so much. At least they have a full team now, though. Did you meet the new guy?"

Dark glasses perched on a straight nose flashed through Finn's mind. "It's a woman. And no. I only caught a glimpse of her. Caster seemed to like her. Said she appeared more than competent."

"I wouldn't expect less from someone Jedynak hired."

"Me, either. Tell me more about your case against Gonzales." Finn didn't want to focus on the pretty magistrate. He was sure he'd learn more about her as the days went on. Right now, though, he wanted to talk about why he was sitting in Nick's office. "What happened?"

Nick blew out a short breath and sat back. "The city arrested a low-level dealer a couple months ago. The man wanted out of the life, having only gotten in it to pay off some of his kid's medical bills, but then he couldn't get out. The city prosecutor's office called me, wanting to know if I wanted to interview him. That was a no-brainer, so I sat down with the guy, and he sang like a canary. Suddenly, I had intel up to my eyeballs about stash houses, the distribution network, even some of the major players." He held up a finger. "He never mentioned Javy Gonzales. I'd have called you if he did." He lowered his hand. "Anyway, we set up a sting on one of the houses the informant mentioned. Undercovers went in, made some buys, and just as we were getting ready to move in, this fancy car rolls up and out pops Gonzales."

"Lucky." Finn shook his head. He wished some of his perps dropped into his lap like that.

"Yeah. Tell me about it. So, I'm in the surveillance van, screaming at everyone to hold their positions. Let him get into the house and see why he's there. He walks in, and the guy one of our operatives was talking to goes over and opens a wall safe and takes out a wad of cash and a bag of cocaine. Gonzales takes the cash and looks at, then asks where the rest is."

"Why was he picking up cash from a stash house? Someone at his level has people to do that for him."

Nick shrugged. "Not sure, but from the conversation that followed that statement, I think he believes someone's been stealing from the organization."

"And with the power vacuum created by Herrera's arrest, he's probably trying to assert some extra authority."

"Exactly." Nick nodded once, and a smile tipped up one side of his mouth. "Except he picked the wrong day and the wrong house to do it."

Finn let out a snort. "That's for sure."

"So, am I forgiven for screwing up our original plan?"

With an overly dramatic sigh, Finn nodded. "I suppose." He chuckled. "Do you think he'll roll to save himself?"

Nick shrugged. "Maybe. We tried questioning him early this morning, shortly after booking him, but his lawyer wouldn't let him talk. He looked pretty dejected, though. With the evidence we have on him, he knows he'll lose at trial. I expect him to cut some sort of deal in the coming weeks."

Excitement created a buzz through Finn's body, waking him up some. They might not get Herrera out of the deal, but they could dismantle a significant portion of the Vargas-Ruiz cartel in the area with Gonzales' arrest. "Awesome. I'll get a hold of his attorney and make a formal request to do an interview." He stood. "Keep me posted on your end of things."

"I will. Hey, what did you learn at Herrera's discovery hearing? I wanted to go, but with the bust last night, time got away from me."

Finn's mouth flattened, some of his elation waning. "His lawyer's pushing hard to discredit Piper. The trial's going to be a rough one."

Nick's expression matched his. "I was afraid of that. Without her testimony, we don't have much. Just the break-in and armed assault at Dr. Tate's. That won't get him much time."

"True, but we have some options. Especially with Gonzales in custody. We might not need her." Finn had a feeling Javier Gonzales could be the key to bringing down the organization. The man was in the thick of it and knew all the key players, Herrera included. "I'm going to head back to my office. Gather up what I've got on their gun-running operation and give Gonzales' lawyer a call." He rounded his chair, turning toward the door. "I'll talk to you later."

"Sounds good."

Lifting a hand, Finn left Nick's office, his pace brisk as he made his way to the stairs, unable to stand still and wait for the elevator. He didn't need that coffee now.

About the Author

Ashley started writing in her teens and never stopped. Her first novel, Smoky Mountain Murder, came out in 2016, and she has since published two more series and has plans for more. When not writing, you can find her with her nose stuck in a book or watching some terrible disaster movie on SyFy. An avid baseball fan, she also enjoys crafting and cooking. She lives in Ohio with her husband, two kids, three cats, and one very wild shepherd mix.

Website: https://ashleyaquinn.com

goodreads.com/ashleyaquinn

amazon.com/Ashley-A-Quinn/e/B07HCT4QST

ALSO BY ASHLEY A QUINN

Foggy Mountain Intrigue

Smoky Mountain Murder

Smoky Mountain Baby

Smoky Mountain Stalker

Smoky Mountain Doctor

Smoky Mountain K-9

Smoky Mountain Judge

The Broken Bow

A Beautiful End

Wildfire

In Plain Sight

Close Quarters

Scorched

Light of Dawn

Pine Ridge

Sweetness

Loner

Shark

Katydid

Homespun